Geoff Tristram has been a pro
over twenty-five years, workin
including Embassy World Snooker, The BBC, Tarmac, Carillion, Past Times, Winsor & Newton, Trivial Pursuit and the television show, 'They Think It's All Over!', to name but a few.

He has painted celebrities such as Jonathan Ross, Ian Botham, David Vine, Alan Shearer, Ian Hislop and Gary Lineker, not to mention virtually every famous snooker player that ever lifted a cue. You may even have noticed him at the World Championships on TV, interviewing them as he drew their caricatures!

Geoff has designed many book covers, album sleeves for bands such as UB40, The Maisonettes and City Boy, (remember 'Heartache Avenue' and '5705'?) and postage stamps, notably 'Charles and Diana - The Royal Wedding', 'Lake Placid Winter Olympics' and 'Spain 1982 World Cup Football' editions. He also writes jokes for the marvellously irreverent greetings cards published by Emotional Rescue Ltd. They're the ones with the old black and white photos and the rude new captions added beneath!

Geoff's younger brother, David, is a well-known and extremely successful comedy playwright, so it was no real surprise when Geoff eventually turned his hand to comedy writing, hence this, his fourth full-length novel, featuring the chaotic and accident-prone artist, David Day.

In order to make up for lost time, Geoff has now written four more novels, which follow this dreamy, scatterbrained character as he grows up and eventually gets a real job.

Geoff's family wonders if he will ever do likewise.

# *Novac & Goode*
# *Solicitors*

*P.G. Wood House, Toffe Street, Belgravia, London 4Q2*

Dear Mr Tristram,

It has come to our notice that the name of a character in your latest novel, 'The Curse of Tutton Common', bears a striking resemblance to the name of our client, Mr Stewart Hickman, proprietor of the Stanmore Industrial Estate, near Bridgnorth.

He wishes to point out that he is an impeccable, upstanding pillar of the community and nothing at all like the fictional 'Lord Hickman of Stanmore' in your so-called comedy - an immoral, double-dealing criminal. Other than sharing a surname, and the same chiselled, aristocratic features, the two men could hardly be more dissimilar.

For example; the fictional Lord Hickman is a conceited, womanising scoundrel who has lost his stately home, whereas Stewart Hickman still resides in his stately pile. We therefore request that you change the name of your villain forthwith, or risk a law suit.

We also wish to remind you that this makes a nonsense of your small-print disclaimer, which states that 'any resemblance to persons living or dead is entirely coincidental'. Coincidental indeed! Pull the other one.

We therefore trust that the final publication will feature a villain with a completely different name - we suggest Lucan.

Finally, our client wishes it to be known that Stanmore Industrial Estate is located in the most attractive and convenient location for all types of businesses, to whom he can offer first class factory and warehouse accommodation for rent on the most competitive terms.

Yours Sincerely,

*Sue Yarassov*

Senior Partner.

# THE CURSE OF TUTTON COMMON

Geoff Tristram

To Celia,
Love Geoff Tristram
x

First published in 2008 by The Drawing Room Press

(A part of Geoff Tristram Limited)

Printed and bound by Antony Rowe Ltd.

ISBN 978-0-9551428-3-3



*Cover illustration by Geoff Tristram.*

Contact the author on gt@geofftristram.co.uk

**With sincere thanks to the incredibly clever Aileen Fraser for editing my books. Lord knows why she keeps doing it.**

**Maybe she needs a social life.**

Dedicated to Doctor John Firth,

my long-suffering G.P.,

and also to the

hundreds of poor Mackerel that died

to provide the Omega 3 capsules I needed

in order to write this book.

## CHAPTER 1

- April 1978 -

### Percy drops in on Julian

Julian was having a hell of a game trying to get Elton John to bend over. He felt sure that the real Elton would have been far more accommodating. To make matters worse, Elton's bright orange nylon wig had fallen off and skidded across the polished tiled floor, heading for the fire exit at a rate of knots, like a guinea pig hell-bent on freedom. The frustrated curator wiped a bead of sweat from his brow and mouthed a choice expletive. If the real Elton ever chose to wear a wig, and judging by the state of his ever-widening parting it was a possibility, he hoped that the singer would choose something a bit better than the one currently making a bee-line for the door.

Julian had manoeuvred the moth-eaten waxwork as far as the stuffed horse, but after that, progress had been slow. You can lead an Elton John to the horse, but you can't make him bend. It was intended to be an upright figure after all - the thing was built that way. No amount of twisting and coaxing was going to create a realistic hunched-over blacksmith pose, and that was the end of it. Elton would have to push the plough instead.

Julian Bytheway, curator of Stanmore Castle's Museum of Local Life, was not having a good week. In fact, he wasn't having a good year, and the last three weren't anything to write home about, if he was honest, which he was. What made things even more galling was the fact that his older brother, Adrian, was Curator of Antiquities at the British Museum, with a staff of twenty and doing very nicely, thank you, whilst he, Julian, was stuck in the world's most boring museum in a little rural village just outside the Black Country, doing virtually everything himself, and greeting as many as three visitors a day in the peak season.

Most weeks, the waxwork figures (which Tussauds sold on cheaply to museums once they were past their sell-by date) usually outnumbered their flesh and blood counterparts. Julian had four of them. Officially they were the ploughman, the farrier, the glass-blower and the Victorian lady; all supposedly anonymous village folk, but he knew full well who they had been in a previous life. Elton John was easy to spot, even sporting an unconvincing orange wig, with his podgy face and gap-toothed smile. So was the similarly gap-toothed Jimmy Tarbuck, currently tending to his furnace, and Sammy Davis Junior in a smock and pushing the plough was an insult to the meanest intelligence. It was asking a bit much to expect visitors, few as they were, to believe that tiny black ploughmen were a common sight in Victorian times, even if it *was* the Black Country. It just didn't ring true, and the blond whiskers and prolific sideburns did nothing to help either.

It had taken Julian a long time to achieve his first curatorship, and he was grateful to have a foot on the ladder. He'd spent four years at Birmingham University in order to gain his B.A. degree in the history of art, followed by a Master's, and finally a diploma in museum management. If he'd stayed on in education much longer, he'd have risked dying of old age in the University library before he found himself a job. His brother, Adrian, had stayed on even longer and had eventually gained a Professorship. Perhaps, mused Julian, if he'd only done the same, he wouldn't currently be rotting away in this God-forsaken backwater of a place, when London called.

Not that London was the be-all and end-all. He liked the local area and the people very much. They were friendly and funny, and had enough time on their hands to direct passing strangers who were lost, unlike those impatient and un-neighbourly types in the capital. No, the place itself was wonderful, and he had no real desire to leave. It was just the museum he couldn't stomach. He'd applied for a job at Birmingham's Barber Institute, a hidden gem of a gallery that housed countless art treasures by the likes of Van Gogh, Rembrandt and Degas, but no positions were currently being advertised. He'd tried Birmingham Art Gallery too, which boasted a world class collection of Pre-Raphaelite art, but again, with no luck. For the present time he was stuck at Stanmore Castle with Elton, Jimmy and Sammy, and that was the end of it.

The frustrated curator decided it was time for a cup of tea. He headed for the sanctity of his cramped little office and put the kettle on. Julian was an amiable thirty-five-year-old from Oxford who bore an uncanny resemblance to Bamber Gascoigne and wore equally unfashionable bowties or cravats, depending on his whim. His mass of curly blond hair was seldom combed, and if it ever was, the effect was ruined within seconds, due to its owner's habit of absent-mindedly ruffling it up as an aid to concentration. The problem was, Julian possessed the type of hair that, once ruffled, didn't eventually subside like a bad soufflé and settle into its original shape. Instead, it remained dishevelled for the whole of the day, giving visitors the impression that an escaped lunatic was in charge of the museum. His eccentric coiffure wasn't helped by the fact that he had a habit of stowing pencils behind his ears whilst not in use, and they could often find themselves swept up in the maelstrom of his ruffling, the result of which was that they would emerge at jaunty angles from his blond waves like flimsy canoes in a raging torrent.

The good folk of Tutton on Stour, though, had taken this gentle soul to their bosom, and were used to his scatterbrained ways. Indeed, they welcomed anyone who wanted to fit in, unlike certain Yorkshire towns that regarded inhabitants with less than twenty years under their belts as newcomers.

When Julian had answered the advertisement for the post of curator at the small museum, he had checked with his elder brother to see if he had any prior knowledge of the place, fully expecting a negative response, and had been surprised to find that Adrian not only knew of it, but had a few juicy tales to relate about its past. Thirteen years previously, when he was just beginning to work his way up the promotion ladder at the British Museum, he had been approached by a Welsh junior school teacher whose star pupil had come across a stash of priceless documents penned by William Shakespeare, the product of a house clearance in Stratford upon Avon. Adrian had successfully acquired the collection for the museum and been promoted for his deft handling of the sale. The young lad in question, a dreamy individual by the name of David Day, had gone on to become an art student at nearby Wolverhampton, and had kept in touch with Adrian by letter every now and again.

On one such occasion, David had told the curator about Stanmore Castle, which at the time was owned by a Lord Hickman, a less than straightforward character who had employed the naïve and gullible young art student to forge a few of the more expensive paintings from his sizeable collection; notably a Monet and a Botticelli. The crooked Lord had explained that he intended to hang the fakes in the castle, and lock away the originals in a vault to prevent theft and appease his insurers; but in reality, he was hatching a plan to leave his wife with the forgeries and abscond with his mistress and the real pictures, which were his wife's property.

David Day, who somehow seemed to attract mayhem like a magnet and become embroiled in complex situations wherever he roamed, foiled Lord Hickman's criminal plans and helped to get him jailed for seven years for his efforts. This meant that the castle had to be sold, after having been in the Hickman family for more than two hundred years. The lucky new owner was a gentleman named Percy Payne, a sixty-year-old barking-mad eccentric with a hairstyle that resembled an eagle's nest with one large egg in it. His eyebrows were the type that couldn't seem to agree on a mutual direction, and just below them sat a nose so hooked that it was probably possible to open a bottle of beer on it, if one were desperate.

Percy was a wealthy, if unworldly character who had made his money from the family printing business. Virtually every bread wrapper that found its way into a supermarket was printed by one of Percy's presses, but he was not a 'hands on' boss. His deceased elder brother, Maurice, had founded the business, and was the real brains behind it. Percy would merely wander through the print rooms waving benignly or frowning distractedly. He hadn't a clue what the machines did, or why, and he certainly couldn't remember the names of all the staff the way his brother did. On bad days he would even struggle to recall his own. All Percy was really interested in was the countryside, his garden and his Labrador, Bertie, and so, when Maurice shuffled off his mortal coil and Compton's of Birmingham Ltd. made him an offer he couldn't refuse, he didn't, and with the proceeds he bought Stanmore Castle. The castle, however, swallowed his funds quicker than a Glaswegian docker could swallow a pint of beer on a Friday night, and the place was looking a bit run down since the glory days, just before justice caught up with Lord Stanmore, and forced him to swap his stately pile for one of Her Majesty's more humble bed-sits.

The Monets and Botticellis had long since gone, as had the successful vineyard, the domestic staff and the Bentleys. Now all that was left was a house with around eight thousand rooms, all requiring new windows and a coat of paint, threadbare Persian rugs, an awful museum (Percy's brainwave to bring in extra cash) a secretary, a gardener, Julian, and fifty acres of land that were quickly returning to the wild. Add to this an owner who couldn't see the woods that he owned for the trees, and one had a perfect recipe for disaster. Julian, in fairness, was warned about the state of the place by his brother, courtesy of David Day, but beggars can't be choosers, as the old saying goes, and the world wasn't exactly throwing jobs at him, in spite of his exemplary academic qualifications.

It was, therefore, a thoughtful and contemplative Julian Bytheway who sipped at his tea that day, wondering what on earth he'd let himself in for. He'd tried to be enterprising and take on the role of the new broom, once he became fully cognizant of how dire his position was. He'd written to the local schools and societies, offering excellent rates for large parties, but the take-up had been disappointing. When they had read Percy's leaflet about the attractions on offer, it was hardly surprising. There were, as have been touched on previously, the magnificent and dramatically-lit tableaux, namely, in no particular order, Sammy Davis Junior, resting against his old plough eating his plastic ploughman's lunch, with a badly-painted backdrop of rolling fields and a terribly-stuffed magpie eyeing up a bit of plastic cheese. There was Jimmy Tarbuck, suitably dirt-stained and sweaty, standing next to an imitation furnace, and taking a breather from blowing his imitation molten glass. And, last but least, there was Elton at the rear of a pantomime horse with his leather apron, a horse shoe clumsily sellotaped to his left hand, which had, in a previous life, been forming the left-hand half of C Minor, and consequently looked a bit arthritic.

If the Tussauds rejects weren't to a visitor's taste, there was always the modest collection of coins, the 'interesting things Percy found whilst walking with his metal detector', the badly-stuffed wildlife, (courtesy of Malcolm Stevens, local amateur taxidermist) the broken Roman pot set in a tray of sand, and the bottle collection, some with little glass marbles in the neck. The room adjoining the main exhibition space boasted a less than comprehensive collection of skulls, (Badger, Otter, Rabbit, Fox, Chicken and Sheep) a moth-eaten butterfly exhibit and a lady with her waxwork head missing, modelling a Victorian beaded dress.

Julian had only discovered that Shirley Bassey's head had gone walkabout an hour after the children of Brierley Bank Secondary School had paid a visit. It was discovered by an old gentleman in the lavatory pan of Tutton public toilets, gazing up manically at him as he prepared to defecate, but he had failed to report it to the police until some four weeks later, due to his coronary and subsequent hospitalization. Luckily, his attempted law suit had been rejected by the courts on the grounds that Stanmore Castle could not, in all fairness, be blamed for the misdemeanours of visiting children.

Eager to milk his captive audience, Percy had also set up a small gift shop adjacent to the exhibition area. This comprised a range of cut glass, which no one had ever purchased due to its expense, a tray full of very long pencils with erasers at the end bearing the legend, 'Stanmore Castle - a great day out for the whole family', a shelf load of little plastic farmyard figures and a nineteen-fifties postcard collection showing the area's various beauty spots in glorious Technicolor. The display, meagre as it was, was made even more so by Brierley Bank's little horrors, who swept through the shop like a swarm of light-fingered locusts, leaving not a wrack behind and the till empty. Angry letters to the school had thus far succeeded in retrieving the grand total of one pound and six pence.

It was fair to say that the gift shop was not, by any stretch of the imagination, Harrods.

* * *

Julian's tea break was rudely interrupted by Percy, who came dramatically catapulting through the door like a circus performer. He ricocheted off the wall, tripped over a large glass display case full of deceased coarse fish and ended up with his voluminous bald head wedged in the wastepaper basket at the far end of the room.

“Do come in!” sighed Julian, wearing the quizzical expression of one who was well used to eccentric entrances from his employer.

“Damned dog!” replied Percy, prising his head from the bin and struggling to his feet. “Why does he insist on falling asleep in front of doorways? Can you tell me that? The bugger’s going senile.”

“I know,” agreed Julian, “and the trouble is, they’re so hard to spot, these twelve stone Labradors.”

“You’re right. They seem to just blend in with the bloody carpets. Anyway, I’ve been thinking…”

“There’s a first.”

“This museum is a disgrace. It needs a facelift.”

“It needs major life-saving surgery, never mind a facelift. Either that or a flame thrower.”

“Quite!” mumbled Percy. “It’s got no pizzazz! The signage is dull, and the backdrops look like they were painted by a twelve-year-old girl.”

“That’s because they were. Your niece, remember?”

“She’s thirteen if she’s a day, you cheeky bugger. Anyway, point taken. I was trying to cut corners, I admit, but it’s not working. It doesn’t look professional. It doesn’t show off the exhibits to their best advantage.”

Julian looked heavenwards, but only managed as far as the tobacco-stained ceiling.

“Percy, we don’t *have* any exhibits. If you go to my brother’s place, you can see ancient Egyptian treasures, mummies, Etruscan art, Greek statues, Roman artefacts and the jewelled crowns of kings. We, by sharp contrast, have Sammy Davis Junior in a nylon wig. Who would come to see that? Only half of our butterflies have both sets of wings, and Shirley Bassey’s head is stuck down a kharzi in the village, literally scaring the shit out of people. I was seriously thinking of doing the same with her here, when she eventually returns. Visit Tutton's Chamber of Horrors – there's a new twist! We could put Elton's body in a coffin and file his gappy teeth into points."

"Points taken, old son. We're hardly a tourist attraction are we?"

"No, we're not. We're laughing stocks, and talking of stocks, those bastards from the school stole ours. They were seen floating along the canal after the buggers left. Mrs Robinson told me. The point is, yes, the backdrops are awful, and so is the signage, but the real problem is the exhibits. What we really need is something to entice folks into the place; an authentic shrunken head, a piece of priceless treasure, the death mask of Nefertiti, an original Shakespeare manuscript, a Constable painting! We could also do with a café, so that when they've studied the bird's egg collection for thirty-five seconds, they can get a toasted teacake and a pot of tea."

Percy nodded sagely. "I agree with everything you say, old son. We need to speculate to accumulate, and that's why I dropped in just now. I agree the signs and the murals aren't the major concern, but we have to start somewhere. I've been talking to a young artist fellow who comes highly recommended; a local lad, and he knows the castle well. Apparently, he worked here some time ago, before I bought it. Until recently, he'd been working for Dudley Council in the art department, straight out of college, and being a bit on the ambitious side, he took the plunge and became freelance. Unfortunately, he ended up in hospital the day after, and he's currently recuperating at home. Well, it's an ill wind that blows nobody a bit of good, if you follow me. He's going broke already, just sitting there, so I suggested that he could ease his way back into work by doing a bit at the castle, at a heavily discounted rate. It'll just about pay his bills and keep him occupied until he's properly recovered and able to whiz about, visiting advertising agencies and what not."

“Is he fourteen?” queried Julian, somewhat churlishly.

“Twenty-four apparently,” replied Percy, his eyebrows doing a series of strenuous push-ups as he spoke, “and I’m told he’s a very gifted painter.”

“Does he know how many legs a sheep has?” asked Julian, cryptically.

“How the blazes do I know? I presume he does. Why?” countered Percy.

“Your bloody niece didn’t,” whispered Julian under his breath, as he turned to the sink to wash his tea mug. And out loud, he added, “Oh, nothing! When’s this lad coming?”

“Tomorrow at eleven,” smiled Percy, stepping carefully over the stuffed fish and exiting the cramped little broom closet of an office. “I have a feeling things will get so much better after he’s added a few touches.”

The door creaked shut, followed by a powerful thud which shook Julian like a small earthquake, as he stood drying his mug.

Outside, Percy Payne was lying across the hall floor with his head up against the far wall. Had he been conscious, he would have seen his old Labrador, Bertie, sauntering down the corridor with a nonchalant backwards glance.

## David's Lump

"I hope you don't mind my mentioning this, James," said David Day nervously, "but you've been holding my testicles for five minutes now."

Doctor Frith hastily removed his hand. David had recently undergone a hernia operation, and had called on his doctor because of the excruciating pains in his scrotum that came without warning, at all times of the day and night.

"If I put it to you," began the young artist, as he sat gingerly on the edge of the couch, some five minutes earlier, "that up to twenty times a day, without prior warning, someone would try to violently twist your balls off with a pair of rusty pliers, do you think that that might add a little extra *je ne sais quois* to your life?"

The doctor had been very sympathetic. "It's fluid, David; from the operation. It settles at the lowest possible point, which is, in your case, the testicles. The best way to alleviate the pain is to lie back on a bed and push them up, using a folded hand towel, like this. Allow me to demonstrate."

Doctor Frith knew David well, as he knew all the local hypochondriacs. If David had seen a documentary on syphilis, he would have most of the symptoms by the following day. He'd been into the surgery eight times that year already, with suspected prostate cancer, heart murmurs, tuberculosis and several rare tropical diseases, not to mention the concerns about his hair falling out. James Frith, being a conscientious man, never took anything for granted, however. Even hypochondriacs got ill sometimes, so when his young artist friend arrived one day complaining that he'd got cancer of the groin, James asked him to drop his trousers and let him take a look.

"The good news is," he began, "you haven't got cancer of the groin, if indeed there is such a thing. What you have there, old son, is a hernia. Have you done any serious lifting lately?"

He shouldn't have asked.

"Funny you should mention that," replied David. "As you know, I turned freelance recently, and I foolishly took the plunge on the strength of a call from a well-known public relations company from London called Lynette French and Co. They'd heard through the grapevine that I was a bit of a nifty caricaturist, and offered me loads of well-paid work all over the country, at black-tie dinners, car launches and sports events. I was bored senseless at Dudley Council's design studio, so I took the plunge. The first job she gave me was in Scotland – nice and local, eh? I was asked to get special monogrammed drawing paper printed and thirty picture frames made up, and then fly to Glasgow, where a hire car was waiting. From there I had to drive to Royal Troon Golf Club, where a bunch of Tina Marina salesmen were staying."

James Frith looked perplexed. "What on earth is Tina Marina?"

"Ah!" smiled David. "I asked the same question. It is a drink, apparently, and these twenty Yanks had won a week's golfing holiday courtesy of their bosses for shifting gallons of the stuff. Anyway, I fly up, grab the car and arrive at the Golf Club at eleven at night, tired and hungry. Lynette told me that the whole jaunt was a big surprise, and the Yanks would love it. Lynette French and Co. was Tina Marina's P.R. outfit, you see. So I check in at reception and ask the cute receptionist girl where I can find a Mr Rick Clarke, who was apparently the sales manager. 'Och, he'll be the gentleman getting quietly pissed at the bar,' she replied, pointing towards a dishevelled eight-foot-tall man in Rupert Bear trousers and a red jumper. I sidled over and introduced myself, and told him the purpose of my visit, still lugging my thirty frames in a holdall, and do you know what he said?"

James Frith was all ears. He followed his mother for that. He was also listening intently.

"What did he say?"

"He looked me square on and said, 'Look boy,' and I quote verbatim here, so please excuse the language, 'we're golf nuts from the States. We intend to be up and breakfasted by seven, and out on the links until dusk. Then we'll return to the club house, eat dinner and get drunk. In other words, there ain't no room in our itinerary for no God-damned cartoonist, so f*** off.'"

"Bloody hell! That was a bit severe. What did *you* say?"

"I didn't say anything. I did what the man said, in short jerky movements. I went back to my room and turned in. The next morning after breakfast I phoned Lynette, and she went ballistic. I told her I wasn't going to stick around where I wasn't wanted, and she'd have to pay me regardless, especially as I'd had all that card printed and the frames made. She reluctantly agreed, so I drove back to Glasgow, caught the plane and came home. I was sitting on the plane, giggling like a fool about the whole damned situation, when the stewardess came round and asked if I'd like a drink from the trolley, and there, believe it or not, was a bottle of Tina Marina, just staring at me. I said to her, 'I don't want that shit for a start!' and laughed till I was in tears. She must have thought that I was a madman, but..."

"David?"

"Yes Doc?"

"It seems a long time ago now, but didn't I ask you if you'd been carrying anything heavy?"

James knew he had to reel David in on occasions. He'd been known to give the long-suffering doctor an hour's worth of admittedly amusing anecdotes, and then leave the surgery without explaining why he'd turned up in the first place, only to put in an embarrassed phone call a day later to mention, as a kind of post-script, that he thought he had a touch of cholera.

"Ah," smiled David, blissfully unaware that there were twenty-six patients potentially dying in the waiting room. "I was getting to that. The point was, I'd been carrying thirty heavy picture frames around in a giant holdall, which gave me a feeling like a pulled groin. Then, when I got home, I went to the loo, and I must admit, I was straining a bit, as you do, and I felt a little pop - I did say pop, not plop - and that was all. Nothing too terrible."

"And when you were in the shower, you noticed a lump, I presume."

"Exactly, so to cut a long story short…"

"David," sighed the doctor, "it's far too late for that."

And so it was that David was admitted to hospital, to undergo an operation which was far more painful than the problem it was intended to cure.

"Remember, David," warned the doctor, "surgery hurts. You'll take time to recover. They cut through your stomach wall, poke your intestines back in and stitch you up. No driving about in cars and no heavy work. You can do a bit of artwork, but that's all."

After a few days in hospital, being fussed over by his parents, his girlfriend, Suzanne, drove him home for bed rest and a spot of home cooking. The so-called food in hospital, he argued, could defy gravity. One day, as an experiment, he had turned the plate upside down, and virtually none of its contents had dropped off. He was grateful to be home, of course, but the impromptu pliers around the knackers he could do without. Other than these unannounced bouts of torture, however, he was feeling up to a bit of gentle socializing, and the call from the castle's new owner was a pleasant surprise, even if the man sounded as if he'd just escaped from a secure unit. The money on offer wasn't good, by any means, but he'd be spending a few pleasant weeks in a place he had great affection for, and very fond memories of.

It was Stanmore Castle where he'd once forged a Monet so perfectly that Lord Hickman couldn't tell the difference, and he'd spent many a happy hour roaming the grounds, looking at the peacocks, or chatting to Jethro, the lame-brained gardener. Now he'd be returning after an absence of five years, hoping that everything was just as it was, with the exception of Lord Hickman of course - he had no desire to meet up with him again. The very thought of that happening filled him with a nameless fear. It was David, after all, who was solely responsible for getting the corrupt Lord jailed for seven years, so a chance meeting would be a tad awkward, to say the very least. He could well imagine how a confrontation might pan out.

"Oh, erm, hello Lord Hickman. How have you been keeping?"

"Oh, you know, so-so. I've been sharing a cell with a tattooed psychopath who wanted to bugger me each evening after lights out. The rest of the inmates hated me because I was a toff, so they spat greenies into my porridge - you know how it is! Oh yes, and one of them carved part of my ear off with a Stanley knife because he thought I'd stolen one of his roll-ups. All in all, I just kept quiet and kept my nose clean."

"Pleased you don't bear a grudge anyway."

"Absolutely not, old chap. Once I've removed your testicles with this hack saw and rammed them down your neck, we can consider the matter closed."

David shuddered at the thought. He had always suffered from a particularly vivid imagination, but he reminded himself that the possibility of meeting up with his nemesis was indeed slight. The man still had two years of imprisonment to serve, and he didn't own the castle anymore; besides, there was nothing to lure him back to the Midlands. His wife had divorced him and he had no offspring. He was about to abscond to Australia just before the police caught up with him, so maybe he'd still want to emigrate and start a new life.

No, David was fairly relaxed about things. Certainly, the castle would still house a few ghosts, but as long as the current Lord Hickman wasn't there, he'd cope.

## One Lord a-Leaping

Lord Hickman of Stanmore, Charles to his friends, (which were, unfortunately, fast becoming an endangered species) lay on his prison bed reading Country Life and sipping tea, for this was not the kind of prison one hears about that is largely populated by one-eyed, scar-faced thugs. He had briefly been ensconced in just such a hell hole, namely Winslow Green, but was quickly moved on, away from the riff raff, before someone decided to ventilate his torso with a stiletto in an attempt to disprove a theory about the colour of an aristocrat's blood. The common-or-garden criminal was generally not over-fond of the upper-crust variety and tended to pick fights over trivial matters, such as the pronunciation of 'off' as 'orf' and suchlike.

After his token spell in purgatory, it was thought best to move His Lordship to a cushy open prison down south, where he could be amongst his own kind; the crooked accountants, bent barristers, dodgy doctors and unscrupulous company directors that one often hears about on a regular basis in newspapers such as the Daily Mail. Here, he could take a shower without fear of molestation, or stroll the exercise yard, happy in the knowledge that no one with a name like 'Cosher Magoo' or 'Scalpel Sid' was about to slit his gizzard, just for the fun of it. Why, he had even found himself a few useful contacts for when he got out, though he drew the line at referring to them as friends. Charles Hickman didn't really go in for friends as such, though he was very good at allowing his victims to *think* that they were. Most of them were drawn to a title like moths to a flame, even when they were aware that the holder of said title was a scoundrel. Somehow, that just added to the mystique, and Charles knew exactly how to exploit their shallowness and stupidity.

Time had gone very slowly for him in prison, but he had kept himself physically fit in the well-equipped gymnasium, and mentally fit by reading the classics, doing the Times crossword each day, and going to art lessons. He was not, by any stretch of the imagination, a talented artist, but he did appreciate fine painting, and especially the Italian Renaissance. He had owned quite a few paintings and drawings from the period, before 'that long-haired little shit' had deprived him of both them and his precious freedom. In fact, it was David Day that kept Charles going, on those inevitable days when everything seemed bleak and pointless, when the hours seemed like weeks and the weeks seemed like years. On these days, Charles would simply lie on his bed, pondering the exact nature of his revenge, and draw some strength from that. Now, after five years of keeping his head down and being a jolly good boy, his patience had finally been rewarded. He was to see the governor, the aptly named Reverend Arthur Godisgood, at eleven that morning, for the results of the parole board meeting.

Cometh the hour, cometh the man, or rather one of his warders, namely - for those who gain some form of satisfaction from knowing these things - Hubert Holden, a mentally negligent, greasy-haired, spotty-faced creature in his mid-thirties. He unlocked the cell door and asked Lord Charles to accompany him on the short walk to the Reverend Godisgood's den, just down the corridor.

The one thing Charles really disliked was having to be subservient and polite to characters like Hubert, whom he considered to be just one degree up the social scale from Neanderthal man. It was on par with having to be courteous to motorway police when one was pulled over for doing ninety-seven in a seventy zone, and being forced to endure their patronizing schoolmasterly drivel and pedestrian sarcasm. What happened to respect for the aristocracy? A hundred years previous, they'd have been tugging at their forelocks and saying, 'I beg yer pardon milord, I didn't know it were thee,' and backing away, bowing furiously as they went. Charles had learnt to bite his lip and suffer it. Patience, after all, was a virtue. There would be plenty time to get his own back, once he was free.

The Reverend Godisgood sat behind a large polished desk, on which was placed an oversized polished wood cross mounted on a plinth. The governor liked his polished wood, and virtually everything in his office seemed to be constructed from it, except the coffee cup he was currently sipping from. That was ceramic, with a detail from Leonardo's 'The Last Supper' printed on it. As Lord Charles was beckoned to sit down on the Spartan polished wood prisoner's chair in front of the desk, he briefly toyed with grasping the heavy wooden cross and bringing it crashing down on the old coot's head, but the moment passed, and reason was restored to its throne.

"Ah, good morning, Lord Charles!" beamed the governor. "And for once, I think you will agree with me that it *is* a good morning. I have here the results of our board meeting, and, to be brief, I can deliver the news you were hoping for. From Monday morning at nine o'clock, you will be allowed to leave this prison on licence. I have to admit that your behaviour has been exemplary whilst you have been here, if one ignores the occasional vitriolic remark, and this is a credit to you. We would all like to think that you have turned a corner, largely due to my bible classes I may add, and we fully expect that you will now be able to return to society and contribute positively to it, rather than milk it for all it is worth, your habit of old. You were born into a noble family, and it is your duty to provide the moral backbone to this wonderful country of ours. If I were you, I would make a fresh start and set about dedicating your life to noble causes as atonement for what you have done."

"Thank you very much, sir," smiled Lord Hickman, with as humble a voice as he could stomach. "I do indeed intend to make amends for my descent into criminality. I have learnt to paint whilst inside, but I will be sticking to my own original work. After what I've been through, if I never saw another forged old masterpiece for the rest of my life, it would be okay by me! I have also read and re-read virtually every book on the Renaissance that the prison library could provide, and I wish to dedicate myself to studying art when I get out. Who knows? Perhaps I could find a job as a museum guide, maybe even in Florence. As you know, I no longer have any money, and I have lost my stately home, so I'll need to find employment. Perhaps my title will help in that regard, at least. I have a few acquaintances I need to catch up with, and a museum I'm aching to see again, and after that, I will probably emigrate. If you were to bump into me in six months' time, sir, I doubt that you would recognize me. I'm going to become a new man, and make a new start, exactly as you have suggested."

The Reverend Godisgood was pleased that this one-time conman and commissioner of fake paintings was at last walking the straight and narrow.

"I'm delighted, of course, but when I mentioned about starting afresh, I'm afraid that I meant in Britain, or at least for the next two years anyway. The conditions of your release state that you are freed on licence. That means that you have to report to your parole officer each week, until your sentence is up. Any breach of the rules means that you could have the licence revoked, and you could find yourself back in here, doing the full stretch, and then some. I also need to inform you that you are not allowed to go anywhere near Stanmore Castle for any reason. Your wife still lives in the area, though, as you are aware, she sold the castle after your divorce. She has made it abundantly clear that she regards any approach by you as harassment. I understand that you have just enough private money to be able to buy a small cottage or rent an apartment. I suggest you do so well away from the West Midlands. Now, if you don't mind, Hubert here will return you to your cell for the last two days. May the Lord protect and keep you safe in the jungle you are about to re-enter."

Lord Charles stood up and shook the governor's hand. "Thank you, sir. Amen!"

He walked towards the governor's door, and turned, just as Hubert opened it.

"If you will permit me one small act of exuberance, sir," he asked.

"Within reason, Charles."

Lord Hickman leapt into the air and expertly clicked his heels together before landing on terra firma once more. For a split second Hubert appeared to reach for his truncheon but then quickly changed his mind.

"Thank you, sir," smiled Charles. "Lacking in decorum I admit, but I felt it had to be done."

## CHAPTER 2

### First Impressions Last

David Day stood at the impressive oak door and rang the bell. It was five years since he had last done so, and a hundred crazy memories began to flood back. Whoever opened the door nowadays, it certainly wouldn't be Lord Hickman, his filthy rich, social-climbing wife or his snooty French secretary. Perhaps, he mused, it might be Jethro, the young, dim-witted gardener, who had never been on the motorway, ridden on a train, or flown in a plane. However, this didn't seem likely. Jethro didn't have the wherewithal to welcome guests, and probably couldn't even fathom out how to unlock the door. No, it wouldn't be him.

David didn't have a long wait to find out. The door creaked open, Hammer Horror style, and a man with a bald pate and a clown's hairdo, enormous beetling eyebrows and a hooked nose stood grinning at him.

"David, I presume!" said the man, offering a giant, liver-spotted hand. "Percy Payne. Do come in."

They entered the oak-panelled hallway, where David had once sat nervously, waiting to be interviewed by Lord Hickman. It looked a little run-down now, and several paintings were missing, unless his memory deceived him.

"I'll lock the door, if you don't mind," said Percy. "We've had a crazy man from the village turn up a few times, screaming the place down and exposing himself. Some days he's dressed in one of those American civil war uniforms, and he speaks with an American accent. Other days he'll be some other damned loony character. One morning he just turned up naked! It's a shame really, but one can't encourage these people. I've warned Julian about him too, just in case he rears his ugly head again - the madman I mean, not Julian. Look, I must shoot - Bertie needs a walk or he'll do it in the library again - not walk of course, crap, I mean. Julian will be with you in a tick, he's just sorting something out in his office. Meanwhile, I've asked my secretary, Glenda here, to make you a cup of tea."

Glenda had appeared, bang on cue, from one of the many doors off the main hall. She was an unattractive, stocky-looking individual with short, mousey hair. She took David's order and disappeared whence she came, leaving David alone with his thoughts, which, as usual, were many and varied.

His father, Len, had dropped him off at the castle, as David was still unable to drive for medical reasons, and Suzanne was away in Solihull for a week, visiting her parents. His operation scar was sore, and the situation wasn't helped by him having developed a slight cough. Normally, this wouldn't have bothered him unduly, once Doctor Frith had explained that it wasn't the first stage of tuberculosis, but now, every time he cleared his throat, his groin felt as if it were being ripped apart by hyenas. What made matters even worse was the huge bunch of keys in his right-hand trouser pocket. He decided to remove them and see if any could be disposed of. He owned more keys than a rock band's roadie, and he felt sure that most of them were probably no longer needed.

As he fiddled with his key-ring, David became aware of a poppy seed that had become lodged in-between his front two teeth, right at the top, by the gum-line, and for someone who was particularly fussy about dental hygiene this was a major problem. The last thing he needed was for a potential employer to arrive in reception and see some fool grinning back at him with a black seed stuck in his teeth. First impressions last, as they say. He placed his keys on the seat next to him and decided to concentrate on the poppy seed instead. After a few minutes of poking and scraping with his fingernails had failed to dislodge it, he tried again with one of the teeth of his comb, but they were too blunt to be of use. He began to look around for a sharp, pointed object, but none came to hand. Then he noticed the key-ring.

Most key-rings consist of two concentric rings of steel, but David's was slightly different. There was just one ring, with a join. To open the ring in order to add or remove keys, he had to prize the join apart, an action that required considerable strength. To avoid creating a gap with constant use, the manufacturers had designed a sharp spiked 'male' end which slotted into a hollow 'female' end, a little like a lady's hoop earring. This sharp, pointed end would, reasoned David, make an excellent toothpick. He picked the keyring up, shoved the many keys to one side, lifted the ring to his teeth, and pulled at the joint with all his might in order to separate the spike from its sheath.

David had nice teeth, generally speaking. They were even and straight with not too many fillings, and unlike Elton John's or Jimmy Tarbuck's teeth, there were no unsightly gaps, which explained why the poppy seed was wedged so tightly and refusing to come out.

What was once just an insignificant ingredient in a cheese and lettuce bap had now become a thorn in David's side – or, if one appreciates a choice when it comes to analogies - a red rag to a bull. He tried to scrape the top of his teeth, where the stubborn seed was ensconced, but the angle of entry was all wrong and the seed was having none of it. Pulling with all his might, he created a more substantial gap in the ring and lowered his front teeth into it, so that the spike was now facing the right way, leaving him with a huge set of keys dangling from his mouth, like some strange tribal decoration. It was at this point that his tenuous grip on the powerfully sprung steel ring slipped, and it snapped shut like a bear trap, tearing a small hole into his gum in the process.

"Thit!" he cursed, as blood began to trickle down his chin. He struggled to free himself from the vice-like grip of the ring, but his efforts, alas, were in vain. The key-ring had become a permanent fixture. The ends of the ring had punched their way through a tiny gap, where his teeth met the gum, and sprung shut with considerable force. Any attempts to remove them caused a searing pain, and he had no choice but to give up trying.

Panicking now, and sweating profusely, he stood up and began pacing the room, trying to clear his thoughts. It was at this juncture that Julian, his hair all over the place and with two pencils poking out of his head at jaunty angles, walked into the hall, totally unaware that a visitor awaited him, largely thanks to his boss's failure to inform him of the fact.

"Hello. Thorry! Thorry!" lisped David, reddening with the embarrassment of it all. "I've got my keyth thtuck, ath you can thee."

Julian, edging around the room, eyed him with justifiable suspicion. Assessing the situation with lightning speed, he decided that the best policy was to engage the man in polite small-talk. "Oh hi!" he began nervously. "Interesting old hall isn't it? Can you see those holes in the wall over there? Musket balls from the civil war. Fascinating, don't you think?"

David began to panic now. The village madman had obviously got in again, and he was ranting about the civil war, just like Percy had said he might.

"Muthketh you thay?" asked David feebly, his keys swinging wildly from side to side. He began to skirt around the walls now, travelling clockwise, just as the madman was doing, but half a mile per hour quicker, so that he couldn't catch up. Julian eyed him like a hawk, waiting for any quick movements or aggression. It was then that he noticed the obscene bulge in the man's trousers, and it began to mesmerise him, just as a snake is mesmerised by a snake charmer. The increase in pace, though subtle, was having a devastating effect on David. He was beginning to sweat bucket-loads and breathe heavily, when suddenly he let out a scream like a stuck pig and grasped at his sizeable crotch.

Glenda, who had just opened the door and struggled in with a laden tea tray, responded with a blood-curdling scream of her own, threw the tray and its contents three feet in the air and fell headlong over Bertie the Labrador as she did so, neatly catching the teapot on the back of her head as she went down.

Julian, sensing that his assailant was distracted, seized the moment and forcibly shoved the madman through the open door of the store cupboard, locking it quickly behind him. There was an almighty crash from within - signalling the demise of three more taxidermy cases - and then, silence. He turned to survey the aftermath, and there was, as he suspected, quite a lot of aftermath to survey. Glenda was lying prostrate with assorted tea things scattered around her, snatching a well-earned rest. There was a crazy man currently occupying his storeroom, and the twelve-stone Labrador, miffed about being kicked in the ribs for the umpteenth time, had taken umbrage and careered into the hall table, removing most of the silver-framed family portraits and the table lamp, which had exploded dramatically.

Percy was next to come steaming in, eager to apologize for forgetting to inform Julian about David's arrival, but before he could drink in the situation properly, he was interrupted by the front doorbell. Julian staggered over and opened the door to a dapper-looking gentleman with a briefcase, who introduced himself as the Museums Inspector for the West Midlands area. Behind them, Julian was acutely aware of a series of bangs and screams which were coming from behind the locked storeroom door.

Now in a state of complete mental turmoil, he ushered the perplexed inspector through the hall at something approaching twenty miles per hour, past the offending storeroom and into the library, offering some lame excuse for the noise, which he blamed on the builders. He sat the man down and asked him if he would like tea, remembering as the words left his lips, that Glenda was unconscious in the hall with most of the tea-making equipment strewn around her.

Percy followed them hot-foot into the library to see what on earth was happening, but was promptly shoved back into the hall, quickly followed by Julian, who slammed the door behind him, in order to cocoon the inspector in a relatively stress-free zone, thereby allowing the curator a few precious seconds to marshal his thoughts.

"I forgot to mention…" began Percy.

"Not now please!" begged Julian, his eyes wild and unfocussed. "Listen! The madman you warned me about got in, and I've locked him in the store - that's the noise you can hear. He's going ballistic. Glenda's unconscious I'm afraid. The bloody loony frightened her to death and she fell over the blessed dog - ah, good, look, she's coming round. The bloke at the door was the museums inspector – he's the man who's now in the library - and the last thing we need right now is some damning report from him. We've got to think fast!"

"Shit!" gasped Percy. "So what's happened to David Day? I hope he hasn't been frightened off by the bloody nutter."

"Who the hell's David Day?" asked Julian breathlessly.

"You know, the artist I told you about. He was here when I left, and I was en-route to tell you he'd arrived but I got side-tracked as usual. Where's he gone?"

The storeroom door sounded as if the hinges were about to come off. A voice screamed from within.

"Mithter Payne, ith that you? That madman you warned me about; I've jutht confronted him, and he locked me in thith bloody broom clothet!"

Percy looked at Julian, who in turn, looked at Percy. The young curator's face drained of colour. They strode over to the storeroom and Percy spoke quietly to the closed door.

"David, is that you in there?"

"Who do you think it ith, Daffy Duck?"

"The voices *are* similar," sighed Julian, ruffling his hair in an anguished way. He pulled the key from his worn corduroy trousers and unlocked the door. David came blinking out of the darkness, his huge bunch of keys swinging from side to side. The floor behind him was littered with badly-stuffed carp, a weasel attached to a branch and lots of broken glass. On spotting Julian, he flinched and took a step back.

"You're *not* the madman, are you?" he eventually conceded.

Glenda was on her knees now, rubbing her head.

"No, I'm the curator. You're not the madman either are you? I'm *so* sorry, it's just that...."

"It'th okay. I admit, to the uninithiated, I would have appeared mad, what with the keyth and the thcreaming."

"...and the bulge."

"Oh yeth. Well I can exthplain all that. I've got a hernia."

"Jeez! It's a big one."

"No, it'th better now. That'th jutht padding."

"I see. I feel this will need more than a cursory skim over, explanation-wise. Shall we all have a nice cup of tea in the library and try to appear as normal as possible in front of our guest? Glenda, if you're up to it, could you do us all a nice cup of tea? I'll understand if you're not."

Glenda said she'd do her best. She staggered off to the kitchen, rubbing her head.

"On second thoughts," mused Julian. "You look a bit unusual with a massive bunch of keys stuck in your teeth. Why not have a rest in the sitting room over there while I go and butter this bloke up for five minutes. Perhaps Percy here could try to remove your key-ring while you're waiting. I can't wait to hear how that happened."

Julian left them to get acquainted, coughed a polite cough, tapped the library door and entered.

The Museum Inspector was sitting on the leather chesterfield leafing through a copy of The Tatler. On spotting his host at the door, he stood up. He had no trousers on, and he was holding his large and over-excited member in his left hand.

## Chapter 3

## Hitler

"Who would have thought that it would have needed the fire brigade to remove your key-ring?" mused Julian, nibbling reflectively on a chocolate Hobnob.

David winced. "We didn't exactly get off on the right foot, you and me, did we?"

"Bloody funny though, thinking back on it!" smiled Julian. "It was Percy's fault, filling our minds with all that madman stuff, and there I was, letting the bugger in, while I was distracted with *your* crazy antics."

"If you'd have had your wits about you," David continued, "you'd have realized he wasn't all the ticket. The high heels were a bit of a giveaway for starters."

"I was too busy thinking about your huge groin and your priceless key collection."

"And what exactly *is* a Museum Inspector for the West Midlands anyway? I've never heard of one before. Have you?"

Julian was wincing now. "No, and I should have been aware of such things, being in my line of work. He caught us napping and it was really embarrassing. I've informed the local bobbies to keep an eye out for him from now on, the bugger."

David took a sip of tea and started to giggle. He had always been a prolific giggler, since he was a small child. He got it from Ruby, his mother.

"How's Glenda?"

Julian affected his best concerned face, which turned quickly to snorts of uncontrollable laughter. "Oh, she's okay; a bit of a nasty bump on the head, that's all. Funny though, I'll swear she's got even more macho since the accident. She's just had her hair cut, and she looks like a bloke with tits."

As the two sat in Julian's cramped little office, bonding against all the odds, the door creaked open a few inches, and a small black and white cat sidled in, wrapping itself around David's legs.

"Did I ever introduce you to Hitler?" asked Julian.

"What, in a previous life?" asked David, who was beginning to think that he had been right after all about Julian being a madman.

"No, Hitler the cat. I call him Hitler on account of his little black moustache, see?"

David stroked the little creature and smiled. It had indeed got what appeared to be a perfect little square moustache beneath its pink nose. "Hitler is a tad harsh. You could have called him Chaplin."

"I much preferred Hitler to Charlie Chaplin. He never once made me laugh. I thought Hitler was funnier."

"Hitler wasn't renowned for his humour, Julian, I think you'll find," said David, seriously worried about his new colleague's morality.

"No, I thought the *name* Hitler was funnier."

"Oh, right! The trouble is, if I ever had to call the cat, especially in public - and you never know when the occasion may arise - I'd be a bit self conscious about shouting 'Hitler, Hitler, come here Hitler'.

Julian pondered this. “You could call him ‘H’ I suppose. I bet Himmler called the Fuhrer ‘H’. And I reckon Hitler would have called Himmler ‘H’ as well, which would have been confusing.”

David was warming to the topic now. “I wonder if he had that little moustache when he was a baby - the real Hitler I mean. I can’t imagine him without it. Anyway, I hate to reel you in, but I reckon Himmler would have probably called him Adi. That’s what Germans call the unfortunate sods who were christened Adolf, for short. Did you know that’s where the name Adidas came from? It stands for Adolf Dasler. You wouldn’t buy their trainers if they were called ‘Adolfs’ would you?”

Julian’s head was spinning. He’d finally found someone with a butterfly mind to compare with his own. “Anyway, this little pest is called Hitler, and, if anything, he’s more trouble than the real Hitler was.”

Julian, as David was fast finding out, was prone to exaggeration.

“How can such a cute creature cause trouble?” asked David. “He looks lovely.”

“He’s a little bastard. He’s always bringing stuff out of the garden and dropping it at your feet. Frogs, baby birds, you name it. It’s horrible. I reckon he’s in league with Malcolm the taxidermist. Yesterday, he dropped a couple of black beads at my feet, which was intriguing. I couldn’t figure out where he could have got them from. Then I realized he’d been having a go at Headless Shirley Bassey and ripped about a foot off the bottom of her Victorian beaded dress. He’s bloody ruined it. Another exhibit knackered.”

David toyed with asking who or what Headless Shirley Bassey was. His original diagnosis about Julian being a madman was spot on, he concluded. He just wasn’t the particular madman David had originally thought he was.

Percy popped his head around the door.

"Ah, nice to see you two getting on after a ropy start. Listen, I've been thinking…."

"Quick Dave, grab a camera," grinned Julian.

The latest in a long line of the catty curator's snide remarks floated by unnoticed several yards above Percy's bald head. "I think some of the display stuff about the English Civil War would look nice done in calligraphy and then blown up in size, don't you?" he asked.

Julian begrudgingly had to admit that this was indeed a good idea.

"I can do calligraphy!" said David excitedly. When I was eleven, I had a calligraphy set that dad got me, and I forged some Shakespeare manuscripts onto tea-stained paper, which makes it look old. When they were finished, you couldn't tell the difference."

"I heard about that from my brother, Ade - not to be confused with Adi," said Julian. "I've been meaning to tell you this, but what with one thing and another I forgot. I've actually been informed about your exploits as a young boy. The British Museum curator who handled the sale of those rare Shakespeare manuscripts you came across all those years ago is my elder brother, and he told me all about you. How about that for a coincidence? I hope you sold him the originals and not your schoolboy fakes!"

David sat open-mouthed in amazement. "YOU are Adrian Bytheway's brother?"

"The very same; the younger, better looking one. You are quite a lad, if all he said was true. Percy here tells me you were also responsible for forging Monets and Botticellis here at the castle five years ago, which, in a round-about way, resulted in Lord Hickman getting sent to jail. Not only are you talented, but there's never a dull moment eh?"

David flushed red. “I just seem to attract madness and mayhem. I can’t help it.”

Percy put his arm around David’s shoulders. “Well old son, we’ve had enough madness here this week to last a lifetime. Let’s hope we’re done with that now, so we can get this museum up to scratch.”

“Would you like me to do your calligraphy then?” asked David, keen to get started.

“Ah! I didn’t realize that it was your bag, old son. I asked Gillian at the library if she could do it, because I thought you’d be more gainfully employed working on the murals.”

Julian looked heavenwards and sighed, not for the first time. If he were to stand a chance of getting this awful museum shipshape, he’d need to confront his employer about these cut-price craftsmen.

“Is this Gillian any good?” he asked wearily.

“Well, she has a nice calligraphy set apparently,” beamed Percy earnestly.

“Oh, well that’s alright then.”

“Mind you, I’ve asked her to do me a sample before I commit myself,” added Percy. “I didn’t want a repeat of the niece’s murals scenario. I’ve asked her to write three titles and a small paragraph, and we’ll make a joint decision when we’ve seen it. Fair enough?”

“Now you’re getting the idea,” said Julian, pleased that his comments about professionalism were finally getting through. “What have you asked her to write?”

“Oh, any old thing. I gave her our three names for titles and I said she could copy a chapter from one of her library books.”

“Fair enough,” agreed Julian, “and now I think I’ll show David here around the exhibits, such as they are, and get him started on some nice professional backdrops. You can't make a silk purse out of a sow's ear, Dave, but I'm afraid you and I will have to try."

"I'll leave you to it then," said Percy. "If that cat's annoying you, I'd throw her out."

"Her?" asked Julian. "It's a her, not a Herr?"

"Yes," replied Percy. "It's a female, why?"

"Oh nothing. Come on then Hitlerina, bugger off!"

After a brief tour, David had to agree that Stanmore Castle's Museum of Local Life was not the most exciting museum he had ever visited. He could certainly make the best of a bad job, but what was lacking was a crowd puller or two.

"You know, Jools," he said, after a few minutes of thoughtful silence. Quite often the best ideas are staring you in the face, and you just can't see them. That's what I'm feeling about this place. A museum of local life just won't pull in the crowds. This castle is steeped in history and intrigue. We need to tap into that, not display Elton John in a smock, shoeing a bloody horse."

"I agree," replied Julian, "and I reckon what you've just said could be the catalyst for something much better. We need to research who lived here from day one, and what they got up to, and maybe there's a display we could make out of that. The castle was owned by the Hickman family for two hundred years. Why don't I dig up some info on them and see if there were any characters amongst them? If the last Lord Hickman was anything to go by, his ancestors should prove to be good reading!"

"There's your homework then," laughed David. "Meanwhile, I'll begin by sanding these walls and emulsioning them to cover up his niece's handiwork. Then I'll pop to the library and find some good artist's reference for the blacksmith's shop and so on. I'm okay to carry on for a few days, but I'm off to Germany at the weekend. Lynette French, the public relations company, have booked me to draw caricatures of the invited guests at a big central-heating exhibition in Frankfurt and the money's good. I'll be back for Tuesday though. And don't worry, I'll take it very easy and there are no heavy picture frames to carry!"

For the next two days, the museum was a hotbed of industry. David had visited the library as planned, and been helped by a rather pretty librarian to gather up several useful reference books. He sketched out his ideas onto the whitewashed walls, and after universal approval and much enthusiasm from Julian and Percy, began blocking in the undercoat layers of his murals, fuelled by gallons of tea and chocolate Hobnobs. After a hard but productive Friday, he washed his brushes out, bade farewell to his employers and headed wearily for the front door. He was flying to Frankfurt first thing on Saturday morning, and was scheduled to work at a three hour VIP champagne reception, after which his time was his own until Monday morning, when he was due to fly home. He was wondering to himself if Lynette French would ever manage to arrange a job for him in Birmingham, when he noticed an envelope lying on the tiled floor of the hall.

At least, it had, at some stage, been an envelope. Now it was a chewed up, soggy mess. He bent down to pick it up, just in time to see a sheepish Labrador exiting stage left with bits of paper still attached to its slobbering great mouth. The envelope was in a poor state, with whole sections missing, but with luck, he hoped the important details might still be readable. He gingerly opened it, trying desperately to avoid touching Bertie's revolting spittle, and fully aware that this might have been someone's private correspondence.

He removed a sodden fragment of cream notepaper and scanned it briefly. It read:

*y David.*

The 'y' was obviously the last letter of a previous word, but the bit before and after 'David' were probably still in Bertie's mouth. He read on:

(missing word*) y love for you is intense. You are all I exist for* (large chunk of paper is missing)

*You must know that we are soul mates. I ache for you to touch me* (slobber has dissolved the next few words) *and feel you inside me.* (torn bit) *together, naked, as we were intended* (another tear) *like a volcano.* (dissolved words)

*Love, your librarian. XXX*

David gathered up the soggy epistle and rammed it into his pocket. His head was swimming. He was not used to being the object of a woman's affections, and at first it wouldn't sink in. The girl had been pleasant enough, but there was nothing in her demeanour to suggest anything more than civility. Some females, he mused, must seem this way on the surface, but simmering just beneath are emotions of ferocious, volcanic intensity. Had the boot been on the other foot, and he'd have been a pretty young girl encountering David Day for the first time, might he not have been similarly affected? He thought long and hard, and concluded that he wouldn't. That said, everyone was different. He may not have been classically handsome, but he did have a cheeky boy-next- door appeal, he thought. After all, his gorgeous fiancée had seen something in him; otherwise she wouldn't now be his gorgeous fiancée. Perhaps he was far better looking than he gave himself credit for. Either that or it was the sheer force of his magnetic personality and humour.

The opening words were intriguing. '*y David'*. At first, the spurious 'y' was puzzling, but then all became clear. Bertie had simply chewed off the capital M. This touching sentiment should have thrilled him, but his feeling of elation was now tempered with a note of caution. What if this girl was a fanatic? What if, with her besotted, befuddled mind, she confronted Suzanne and gave it to her straight. These obsessed types could cause misery; he'd heard about such cases before in the local newspapers, where paint stripper had been thrown at fiancée's cars, and their pet hamsters mutilated out of spite. Reassuringly though, the writing appeared calm, and rather beautifully written, rather than the wild scribblings of a deranged mind. He decided to sleep on it and not do anything hastily. He would cool off in Deutschland over the weekend, and decide on his strategy when he got back.

## CHAPTER 4

## Incontinental Airlines

The big black gentleman next to David on the plane had arrived sweating heavily, and had sat down mumbling apologies to all and sundry. He was sorry he was a little late getting on the aircraft, and he was sorry that he was so large. He was also sorry about clonking the lady in front's head with his luggage as he struggled to fit it into the locker, and he was sorry that he was a nervous flyer.

As the plane thundered down the runway, he began speaking in tongues and crossing himself furiously about the chest. Then he produced a small bible from his jacket pocket and began to pray. David, who himself was not a good flyer, was wondering to himself if this man knew something that he didn't.

Now David's own hands were feeling moist, and he began wiping them on his trousers. He hated take-off at the best of times, and this harbinger of doom next to him wasn't helping matters one bit. What also grated was the fact that Mr Nervous was around twenty stone in weight, and was taking up one and three quarter seats. In an attempt to get more comfortable, and to create an inch of clear gap between their two bodies so that the man's sweat didn't seep into the arm of David's coat, David shuffled his bottom towards the window. This was a big mistake. The unseen hand with the rusty pliers connected with his engorged and fluid-filled testicles, causing David to let fly with an ear-piercing, gut-wrenching scream. The effect was dramatic. Mr Nervous clutched at his huge chest in panic, and his protruding eyes rolled hysterically. He began to recite some mantra in an obscure African language, and there was more water coming out of his pitch-black skin than the fountains of Versailles.

The stewardess rushed forward to see what the commotion was all about, but she could get little sense from either party. Trying to explain a severe pain in the testicles to anyone but a man is frankly a waste of time. It is like trying to describe a colour to Stevie Wonder. David simply didn't know where to get in order to relieve the pain he was experiencing, let alone give a running commentary to a concerned female with a trolley. His only consolation was that these episodes of discomfort were usually mercifully brief, and this was what he was praying for. The large black man, meanwhile, was hyperventilating so badly that she considered David's problem to be the lesser of two evils, and concentrated on him, which suited the young artist perfectly. Right now, like Marlene Dietrich, he just wanted to be left alone.

After a few minutes, the young lady had calmed the man down by getting him to go through a series of breathing exercises. As soon as he was able, he then politely requested to be moved to another seat, much to the chagrin of the twenty or so passengers who had managed to secure a row to themselves. As Mr Nervous and his hostess walked unsteadily down the aisle, they virtually all developed a fascination for the wonderful aerial views of Britain, and sat with their noses glued to their portholes, hoping not to be chosen. David was especially pleased to observe that the short straw had gone to the ill-mannered double-glazing rep from Sutton Coldfield who had jumped his place in the check-in queue. Perhaps the Buddhists were right about karma after all.

After an eventful start, calm gradually descended on the aircraft once the dinner was served, and David was able to sit and ponder the remarkable letter that he had received. He had to own up to feeling a frisson of excitement about the situation, but he still had no clear idea of how to handle it. One wrong move, and his wedding would be off, and he most certainly didn't wish for that to happen. The other man's bread was always greener, but David knew which side his grass was buttered on, as his grandmother, Bertha, had once so eloquently put it. He decided to shelve all thoughts of pretty librarians, and instead, occupied his time with the in-flight magazine and a chunk of grey rubber chicken. After lunch, his eyelids began to feel heavy, and he drifted off into a light sleep.

He was rudely awoken by two completely different but simultaneous stimuli. The first was a message from the captain, stating that landing would be in ten minutes. The second was a feeling that the whole world was about to fall out of his bottom within the next three seconds, unless he did something about it. The 'fasten seatbelts' sign had come on, and passengers were no longer able to visit the toilet. Glancing around him, and noticing that the stewardess was pre-occupied with trying once again to calm the large black gentleman ten rows back, David slipped off his seatbelt and sneaked up to the lavatory just behind the cockpit, unobserved by the handful of comatose passengers in front of him.

He reached the sanctity of the lavatory with seconds to spare. No sooner had he ripped down his trousers and underpants, a mighty explosion of diarrhoea hit the pan, leaving him feeling unmanned and weak. He could only speculate as to what had caused this sudden outburst, which had arrived virtually without warning. Maybe it was simply a case of nerves, caused jointly by the flight, the job he was about to do in Germany, and the influence of the large black gentleman. Perhaps the answer lay in the grey rubber chicken. Whatever had caused it, the only adjective that went anywhere near describing the resulting mayhem was 'spectacular'.

David tried to compose himself and attend to his toilet, but just as he stood to exit the cubicle and resume his seat, an awful, stomach-churning feeling came over him again, and he was forced to rethink his plans. The second wave was every bit as forceful as the first, and the after-shock prevented him from doing anything more active than staring at the wall and groaning quietly.

Outside, David could hear the stewardess strapping herself into her bucket seat in readiness for landing; he could also hear the 'thunk' of the mighty wheels popping out of the undercarriage. Desperately now, he struggled to his feet and began to fasten his trousers up with trembling hands, but as he did so, he knew another batch of the unspeakable liquid fertiliser was on its way. He unbuttoned his trousers and reluctantly prepared his own undercarriage for yet another landing.

The third consignment was, if anything, even more dramatic than the first two had been, causing David to shriek with pain as his operation scar was tested to the full.

Outside, the stewardess began to bang on the door.

"Is there someone in there?"

"Yes."

"You shouldn't be in there. You were told not to leave your seat!"

"I know, but I didn't have much choice."

"Are you the man who screamed the place down earlier?"

"Erm, yes, but......"

"Excuse me. I need to tell the captain he can't land."

The gamut of emotions ran through David's head as he heard the stewardess leave her seat. He was feeling very weak, and every time he endeavoured to rise, he was forced back onto the lavatory. As a side issue to all this, he was trying to figure out why the lady had said the captain couldn't land the plane. At this precise juncture, he felt the aircraft rise sharply, causing him to jettison another load of waste material with some haste.

Within seconds, the stewardess was back with more facts.

"Listen sir. We are not allowed to land a plane with a passenger stuck in the loo. It's against regulations. The captain has pulled up and he's circling the airport. He's missed his slot now, so we'll have to stay in what we call a holding pattern until air traffic control tell us it's okay. Can you come out now please?"

"No."

"Why not?"

"I'm not saying."

"You have to come out right now."

"I've shit myself."

"Oh!"

The captain's voice came over the loudspeaker system.

"Ladies and gentlemen, this is captain Broadbent speaking. I'm sorry to inform you that someone is in the lavatory, which means we cannot land at the moment. We have also missed our slot, meaning that we may have to keep circling until we are given clearance. May I, on behalf of Inter-Continental Airways, apologize for the rail connections, taxis and important meetings you will probably have missed, thanks to the idiot stuck inside the toilet. If it's any consolation, we have also lost out, to the tune of hundreds of pounds worth of aviation fuel, not to mention the delays this will cause for the rest of the day as we try and play catch-up. Thank you."

The stewardess tapped the door.

"Sir, are you able to come out yet?"

David placed his very flushed face against the metal door and hissed, "I hope I am, but do you really think that I'm going to come out of here and swagger back to my seat with that lot baying for my blood? You have to be joking. They'll kill me. I'm not coming out unless you pull that blue curtain across and let me hide somewhere."

"I'm afraid that's not possible, sir."

"Well I'm staying put then."

There was a short silence, which David interpreted as a deep and meaningful discussion with the powers that be.

"Sir, very well, the curtain has been drawn."

David, ashen and shaking, sheepishly opened the door and was met by the stewardess, who was trying her best to look stern, but missing it by a mile. She ushered him to a bucket seat next to her and strapped him in, after shutting the lavatory door for fear of poisoning the whole plane. David had had some embarrassing moments in his life; in fact, far more than virtually anyone alive, but this took the biscuit. He wished he could have worn blinkers like a race horse, to avoid eye contact. Coupled with this, he still felt awful. All he could do was drift into a world of his own, and hope that he could last till the lavatories in the baggage reclaim area.

Ten minutes or so later, the plane had taxied into Frankfurt Airport and the doors were opened. As the passengers shuffled off, they glanced over to the forlorn figure hunched in a fold-down chair, whose gaze appeared to be fixated on a large rivet in the wall to the side of him. The large African gentleman mopped his brow and called out, "God be with you, brother." The double glazing rep from Sutton Coldfield paused at the exit and decided to add his own message of sympathy.

"Wanker!"

* * *

After reclaiming his bag and making one more dash to the lavatory, David headed for the airport pharmacy. Thankfully, he had studied German at 'O' level, and could still remember a little. He staggered to the counter with his trolley and caught the eye of the assistant.

"Entschuldigen Sie bitte. Haben Sie etwas für durchfall?"

The young blonde lady smiled and handed him a small packet.

"Welcome to Germany," she said.

He read the instructions carefully, and having ascertained that the word 'zwei' featured in there somewhere, took two tablets on the spot, without even the aid of a glass of water to help them down.

The boss of the firm that he was to draw caricatures for the following day had promised to meet him at the airport and take him back to his hotel. He had also promised a spot of dinner, but at that precise moment, David's thoughts were a million miles from eating. In order to ease the potential identification problem, Herr Klopstein had described himself to David on the phone, prior to the trip.

"I vill be ze short, fat one wiz ze tall hair."

David, though feeling distinctly below par, was rather amused to see, waiting with a placard bearing the legend 'D DAY' a very short, fat German with a hairdo that doubled his height, waiting patiently on the other side of the barrier. Due to unforeseen 'durchfall' (loosely translated as 'through fall' - the Germans have a way with words) David had forgotten to purchase a carnation for his lapel, so instead he waved his arms about like a lunatic. Once through the barrier, Herr Klopstein gave him a manly handshake and fixed his eyes with a kind-hearted, even stare. At least, the intention was so to do, but as David was six feet tall, and the German was only four-feet-nine to the eyebrow line, this proved difficult.

"Hi, Herr Klopstein of Klopstein and Fuchs," he said. "Pleased to meet you!"

"David Day," replied David. "You speak English!"

"Ja, a little, but it is very rusty. Do you speak German, Mr Day?"

"Ja, ein bisschen, aber ich bin auch rostig! Call me David, by the way. I can't stand formality."

"Du sprichst gut Deutsch, David. It's Adi, by the way."

"What is?"

"My name."

Oh, right. Nice name."

The German grabbed David's luggage and they headed for the car park. David had already bored the lederhosen off him on the telephone earlier that week about the delicate state of his groin, so Adi was being the perfect gentleman.

"I sink ve vill drive to ze hotel and haf dinner zere. Normally, I would not, aber zis hotel has gut food, ja?"

"Ich verstehe!" replied David, smugly pleased that he'd remembered his German words, and was therefore able to meet his client half way with their conversation. Adi opened the boot of his large Mercedes Benz saloon and placed his and David's luggage inside. David walked to the passenger door and waited.

"So you wish to drive my car?" laughed Adi. David blushed and walked around to the other door. The German pulled away at a leisurely pace, crossed the river and headed for the suburbs.

"You see zat red brick place over there?" he asked, beckoning to a large building that reminded David of a Victorian mill. "Zis is where ze ladies of ze night live, just in case a young artist gets lonely." He winked horribly and smiled at his guest.

"What? A brothel?"

"Nein, nein! Zat is where zey make soup, surely? Zis is a whore house."

"Nein, ich verstehe gut!" explained David. "The word, auf English, ist 'Brothel'"

"Nein?"

"Ja!"

"Well, zat *is* interesting. I did not know zis! A new word! When we arrive at the hotel, you must write it down for me."

"Where will I be working tomorrow?" asked David. "The Mess?"

Adi laughed. "We both need a little help with ze languages, eh David? We pronounce it 'Mess*e*', because here we sound the final 'e', as in Porsche. Not Porsch. Don't worry. I will write everything down for you at the hotel, so you don't get lost."

The Mercedes pulled onto the car park of the Brucke Hotel and Adi pulled the bags from the boot. David, surprisingly, was feeling up to a little dinner now, and the diarrhoea pills seemed to be working wonders. The two men sauntered into the half-empty restaurant and took a table by the window, overlooking the river. A waiter with an impossibly large moustache took their order for two beers, and was gone.

"So," said Adi, stripping the back off a beer-mat and taking a very expensive-looking fountain pen from his pocket. Show me zis new word."

David wrote BROTHEL and showed it to Adi, whose thirst for knowledge was admirable. Either that or he needed practical information to hand, ready for some impending English trip.

"Your language is very complex," he smiled. "I also haf trouble with Edinburgh. You English pronounce it 'Borough', but it is written 'Burgh', and yet, Market Harborough is pronounced as it is written."

David could offer no explanation, but ventured to suggest that Adi was a teapot calling the kettle black.

"You think *our* language is tough? What about yours? Just try to say a simple thing like, 'I remember your face' in German. 'Ich erinnerne mich an ihr Gesischt.' It's like a tongue twister! And I don't know anyone who can manage 'Das Schloss' after three pints."

"Nonsense!" grinned Adi, sipping at his freshly delivered beer. "German is simple! I know lots of two-year-olds who can speak it. Now give me that beer mat, and I'll show you how to pronounce our place names properly."

The two amused themselves for the next ten minutes until dinner arrived, wrecking beer-mat after beer-mat in an attempt to decide whose language was the most complex. After a simple but enjoyable meal, Adi paid the waiter and made his apologies. He had two small children, and he liked to see them off to bed each night. As he was about to leave, David realized that he still didn't know where to go the following day, and as he was a control freak, and a punctuality fetishist, this was important.

Adi stripped the umpteenth beer-mat of the evening, an action that did not go wholly unnoticed by the moustachioed waiter. He wrote down the address for the taxi driver, and underneath, the time David needed to get there by. Adi was rather impressed with David's almost Germanic obsession with timekeeping. After all, it was important that his guest was there, ready with his pen poised, as the civic dignitaries arrived for the champagne reception. David thanked him for dinner and caught the lift to his room. What he really needed now was to take a shower and get an early night. Hopefully, he would be feeling a lot better the next day, and ready for a gruelling three hour drawing stint.

David's alarm call from reception arrived bang on time at half-seven, but he was already wide awake. The first night in a strange bed always played havoc with his sleep patterns, and he'd been in a half awake, half asleep no man's land for most of the night. His room was far too hot, and he'd spent the first few hours tossing and turning, his mind spewing out nonsense, unable to turn off.

He'd even fantasized about a daring sexual liaison with his library girl in the hope that it would lead to a nice, steamy dream, but the tossing continued unabated, admittedly without as much turning. It was only then that he seemed to drift into a half sleep, in which state he remained till six-thirty.

After a hot shower he popped downstairs for breakfast, returning to his room some half hour later to shave and refill his pens, ready for battle. A visit to the lavatory produced a pleasing, solid result, and buoyed by this, he put his coat on, straightened his tie, grabbed his attaché case full of paper and pens and headed for reception.

The stunning, six-foot-tall blonde receptionist with pigtails and erotic underarm hair called him a cab, and within seconds he was leaping into the back seat and saying good morning to the driver. It is comforting to be surrounded by familiar things when one is visiting a foreign country; it makes one less homesick, and David found himself smiling benignly when the driver turned to greet him. Satnam was from India, and spoke exactly the same way that all the taxi drivers in England did.

"Okay maert, where you vant to go?"

David smiled and handed him his beer-mat. Satnam explained that he was originally from Smethwick in the West Midlands, but had moved to Germany to be nearer to his family, who all drove taxis with the exception of his elder brother, who was a consultant surgeon. He skidded away from the hotel, dodging other cars by margins of at least half a centimetre, and David settled down in the back, as best he could, nervous about his morning's work and of getting killed by Satnam, in approximately equal measure.

The car soon left the suburbs and headed for the bustling city, crossing the bridge once more. Satnam then swung right to follow the river, and turned to David, who was dreamily sight-seeing in the back.

"You here for fun, maert? It's a fun city, nartamean?"

"Some might call it fun," replied David. "It's just hard work as far as I'm concerned."

Satnam frowned and looked quizzical. "I vish I vas doin' vat you are doin', instead of drivin' a taxi all day, you lucky bugger."

David felt he could add nothing to this, so he didn't. He was, however, curious about Satnam's route.

"Is this one of those sneaky long-winded back ways, to avoid the traffic?" he asked, worried that he no longer recognized the landmarks from the day before.

"No, maert. It's the straight way. Boy, can't you vait to start all this hard verk or something?"

A few minutes later, the taxi screeched to a halt outside a drab, concrete building, and David was let out. He paid the driver, who then executed a full three-hundred-and-sixty degree turn in the busy main road, causing untold chaos, and chugged off with thick blue smoke belching from his decaying exhaust. David walked up the steps to the reception, where another gorgeous young lady sat behind a glass desk. Germany seemed to be over-populated with these creatures. Italy was the same. They could all carry off wearing impossibly tiny leather skirts without looking like hookers, unlike the majority of English women. They also seemed to have been poured into leg moulds from the age of three until they reached sixteen, just as American kids were fitted with teeth braces, so that their legs were perfectly formed when they reached adulthood.

The young lady said 'Guten Morgen' and asked his business.

"Hello!" smiled the young artist. "I'm David Day. I'm here for the champagne reception. There's a group of ladies I have to draw, apparently."

The receptionist frowned. "I don't know about any drinks reception here. Are you sure you have the correct place?"

"I think so. It's a group of VIP ladies."

"We have many ladies here. Some of our guests do like to draw them."

David sensed that all was not well. He was quick like that.

"This isn't the Messe is it?"

"No, this is a whore house, if you'll excuse the term."

"Oh shit! I gave him the wrong beer mat!"

"Sorry?"

"Nothing. Can I get a taxi from here, quickly?"

## CHAPTER 4

## A Good Book Improves the Mind

"What on earth did Lynette French have to say?" Julian loved a good disaster story.

"Oh, she told me that I'd never work for her again. My first big client as a freelance and she tells me to sod off before I've even drawn anyone for her. I'm as sick as the proverbial parrot, if not sicker."

"Surely you'd have only missed half an hour with your detour. Couldn't you have explained it to Adolf?"

"That's the bloody trouble," sighed David. "I didn't just miss half an hour. "I missed the entire reception party, thanks to bloody Satnam."

"Who hell he?"

"The bloody taxi driver. The brothel receptionist called me a cab, and who should turn up but Satnam again. I explain that he's read the wrong beer-mat, and he then sets off for the Messe like a bat out of hell. After about two minutes, he gets a flat tyre, so we pull in, and he says, 'won't take a sec, maert'. After about ten minutes, he still can't get the wheel off, and he phones the AA, or whatever they're called in Germany, and all the time my heart's palpitating like mad, and I'm looking at my watch. The AA van turns up, and the bloke can't get the wheel off either, so I say to old Satnam, look, I can't wait, so he calls his brother, who turns up a quarter of an hour later, and I jump into *his* cab. He immediately collides with a tram - I kid you not, Jools - and trashes his car. It's a miracle I wasn't killed, so now I'm nearly an hour late and I'm not there yet. I flag down yet another taxi and scream, 'Messe bitte, und schnell!' and he goes careering off, like in a movie. We were doing well till I let fly with one of my groin-related screams, and he screeches to a halt, asking what's up. The bloke doesn't speak a word of English or German, as he's from Bulgaria or somewhere, and by this time I'm a sweaty mess and I'm shaking, because I'm so late. He interprets this as aftershock from the tram accident and drives me to the bloody hospital for a check up. It was nice of him of course, but I nearly throttled the bastard. I kept saying 'Messe, Messe' and he kept holding his hand up and saying, 'no, hospital, hospital'. I got out of his car and limped all across town and into the Messe, but I hadn't got a clue which hall I was in, and the place is as big as a city. I asked at reception, and they directed me to where they thought it might be, so again, I ran like the wind, or rather, limped like the wind I suppose, shaving seconds off my previous best. Well, guess what? It *was* the right place, and there was an hour left to go, so better late than never, I reckoned. I steamed into the hall, found the delegation and old Adolf, who was looking apoplectic. The trouble was; so was I. For the first five minutes I just stood doubled-up in front of him, red-faced and panting. Eventually, I had enough breath to explain my predicament, and he begrudgingly told me to draw for the last hour."

"So why didn't you?"

"Because all my equipment was in a taxi two miles away, being extricated from the front end of a tramcar."

"Oh!"

"Oh about sums it up."

"Cup of tea?"

"Please."

"What did you find to do till your flight?"

"I'd rather not say. Look, when I've finished my tea, I'm going to pop to the library for more reference. Have you dug up anything interesting about the Hickmans while I've been away?"

Julian smiled an enigmatic, self-satisfied kind of smile. "Not half. Stay awhile and prepare to be amazed."

David drew up his chair. Julian produced a buff-coloured folder from his shelf and dusted it off.

"This was in the attic. Percy's been rummaging around up there all day, and he found this in an old trunk. I've done a bit of digging on the history of the castle, and it's well worth a panel or two in the museum. The usual stuff; Lord Whatsit of such-and-such who was a second cousin to William, Duke of Bobbington, who fought with Edward the Tenth in the battle of doodah and got a sword up the arse for his trouble. To be honest, it's only 'fairly' interesting as ancient history goes - nothing earth-shattering. Then came the Hickmans, who were a nondescript bunch - and here's the good bit - *until* Lord Henry Hickman arrived. Henry was here in and around the nineteen-twenties, and he was a real character; an adventurer, cad, bounder, gambler and explorer. Have I missed any out? No, I think that's it! His real passion in life was Egyptology, and he was out there digging, like every other member of the landed gentry, at the same time as Howard Carter, and not without some success, though of course, Carter stole all of the limelight after discovering Tutankhamun. The only vice Hickman seems *not* to have succumbed to was adultery. By all accounts, he was devoted to his wife, Lady Caroline Hickman, who was a well-known and respected Egyptologist herself. They had a butler called Stokes, and he too seemed to be inseparable from them. It mentions here that a familiar sight in Cairo was Lord and Lady Hickman, dressed in the garb of the locals, waited on hand and foot by Stokes, who was dressed like Jeeves in his black tailcoat, whatever the weather! Apparently, by nineteen-twenty, old Hickman had amassed a huge collection of Egyptian artefacts, which he stored and displayed here at Stanmore Castle."

"So where are they?"

"Ah, well that's the tragedy. I can see now where the current Lord Hickman gets his wayward streak from. Lord Henry ran up massive debts, gambling in London casinos, and there was talk that he'd occasionally had to flee the country to escape a succession of angry creditors. It's all pretty well documented in these old cuttings and letters, but here comes the really interesting and mysterious bit. Are you ready for this? Lord Hickman disappeared off the planet on July the seventh, nineteen-twenty three, just after he'd returned from a very successful trip to the Valley of the Kings. So did his wife, and Stokes, the butler. When visitors called at the castle, it was empty, like the Marie Celeste. It appeared that they'd just vanished off the face of the earth. The creditors arrived to try and claim what was owed to them, but there were no Egyptian treasures to claim. Lord Hickman had done a bunk, and taken his treasure, his wife and his loyal butler with him. The press speculation was that he'd sold his wares abroad and gone to live anonymously somewhere, to start a new life. Weird eh?"

"What, like Lord Lucan?"

"Exactly! And they say history repeats itself don't they? From what you've told me about the current Lord Hickman, he was trying to do the same, until you collared him."

"Good God! You're right. He was trying to flog his treasures to a bent German art dealer called Herr Grunstrasse, so that he could begin a new life down under. You don't think he's the old Lord Hickman reincarnated do you?"

"Come on! I don't believe in the supernatural. It's bollocks! This is merely a case of genetics, Dave - a wayward streak that runs in the family. Here's a picture of him, by the way."

Julian showed David an old sepia-coloured photograph, mounted on a green card that bore the inscription, 'Brown, Barnes and Bell. Photographers to the Queen. Royal Studio, thirty-one, Bold Street, Liverpool', in gold embossed lettering. It showed a noble-looking character in a wing-collared shirt and three-piece suit, staring arrogantly at the photographer, his mouth completely covered by a large, handlebar moustache.

"That's just uncanny," gasped David. "He's a dead ringer for the current Lord Hickman, except that the moustache is larger."

This was all very exciting for David, who was fascinated by the whole Egyptian thing, as, in fairness, most people appeared to be. He also loved the nineteen-twenties and thirties periods, so the mystery unfolding before him was appealing on two fronts.

"Well, we may not have any exhibits," he mused, "but what we *do* have is something we can liven up the museum with. We can tell the Lord Hickman story, and back it up with some great graphic panels about the Valley of the Kings. It's got to be better than Elton John and Co, surely!"

"I agree," said Julian, "but a load of panels and no three-dimensional stuff can be a real turn-off for visitors you know. On its own, it's not enough."

Their conversation was interrupted by Percy careering through the door with a shoebox in his hands, and somehow managing to maintain his balance.

"If it isn't the bloody dog, it's the bloody cat. Morning lads! Look what I've just found in the loft! I've been having a tidy up. You can't beat a good clearout, now and again."

"I know," said David. "I had one on the plane."

Percy handed the shoebox to Julian, who took off the lid. Inside were two small and obviously ancient carved wooden sarcophagus-shaped items with musty looking swing tickets tied around their necks, one bearing the word 'Rametup' and the other, 'Sippahottut'. There was also a decorated wooden comb and a black and white photograph showing what appeared to be Lord Henry Hickman in front of a wall full of hieroglyphics.

"My goodness!" beamed Julian. "What a find! These are called ushabtis. They are the scaled-down models of the deceased person's sarcophagus, which would have been buried alongside the mummy to help them in the afterlife. David, it looks like we have a couple of things to exhibit after all!"

David picked up the comb and ran it through his hair. "What's this then? I presume it *is* a comb of sorts."

"Yes. This was probably the comb belonging to the deceased. Don't you think that's creepy? Some ancient Egyptian thousands of years ago sat on the Nile, preening him or herself with that, and you've just combed your hair with it."

"Who are they though?" interrupted Percy, almost beside himself with delight. "We must find out."

"I can arrange that," smiled Julian. "I'll give my brother a ring and provide him with all the facts. I can photocopy the picture and post it to him. They have blokes there who are fluent in hieroglyphics. They'll soon decipher all this. I'll do it straight away."

"Well I'll mosey on down to the library then," said David. "I was going for some rural life references for the waxworks exhibits, but now I think I'll get a few books out on ancient Egypt. I feel a mural coming on."

Still banned from driving for another two weeks by Doctor Frith, David decided to catch the bus into the village. Luckily, the bus stop was very conveniently situated right outside the front gates of Stanmore Castle, and within ten minutes he was chugging along the country lanes en-route for Kinver High Street. He alighted from the bus and walked up the hill to the little village library, his heart beating a little faster than usual. He approached the main desk, where a rather frumpy little lady in a long dress was busying herself with tidying up great piles of returns behind the counter. She wore huge spectacles with thick brown rims, which gave her the appearance of a timid and short-sighted little owl. He handed in a few books that he'd finished with, and was just about to begin his search for the Egyptian section, when he noticed the pretty librarian in the quiet room, sat at a table with her back to him and her nose in a good book. He quietly pushed open the door and wandered in, still not sure what, if anything, he should say or do. He nervously paced the perimeter of the room, pretending to be interested in books on politics and astro-physics, and then, with a sudden burst of confidence, padded quietly up the his secret admirer from behind.

Mandy Robinson was on her break. She'd made herself a nice cup of coffee, and settled down to read her book, 'True Crime USA'. Mandy had been raised by good Christian folk, and was herself a regular churchgoer, singing each Sunday in the choir with her fiancé, Gerald, a trainee accountant from Wolverhampton. It was, given the salient facts, somewhat unusual for a strait-laced young lady like Mandy to have such an interest in gritty and sensational true crime books, but she was seriously addicted. Not for her the sloppy romance paperbacks favoured by Gillian, the drippy, owl-like creature on the front desk. No, Mandy liked black and white police photographs of real-life crime scenes, with bloated dead gangsters spread-eagled on the floor, riddled with bullets. She thrilled to the descriptions, written by real-life American cops, of who had discovered whom, and in what condition, and lapped up the sections that explained what had made murderers snap, and decide to stab their entire family before turning the knife on themselves. Perhaps her regimented, moral lifestyle had left her craving excitement, and this was how she found it. Whatever the psychology behind it, it kept her happy, and there was no law against it. She was currently engrossed in the chapter on Laurence Leibowitz, the so-called 'Library Lothario' (these publications loved their alliteration) who, before he was executed by lethal injection, had a habit of sneaking up behind unsuspecting library staff in and around

Dallas, Texas, and stifling their screams by clasping a hand over their mouths, before shoving a sharpened ice-pick into their necks and rendering them dead. The defence explained that he had suffered a terrible childhood, caused by his librarian mother running off with a lesbian from Ohio, and a father who regularly 'drank and beat him'. One must presume from the seriousness of Laurence's eventual crimes that the author was not referring to 'tea and chess'.

The timing of David's second encounter with Mandy Robinson could fairly be described as unfortunate for both parties. He had been in two minds about his visit in the first place, as he had been experiencing waves of excitement and guilt in equal measure. Pacing the room behind her, he had just about resolved to walk quietly away, like the shy hero of a corny western, when a sudden impulse saw him change direction and head for the unsuspecting young lady. When one was given the 'come on' by the opposite sex as infrequently as David had been, it seemed downright churlish not to pop along and introduce himself to the girl, enjoy the attention for half an hour and then let her down as gently as he could, leaving a door open, should Suzanne ever tire of his charms.

"Who knows?" he asked himself as he approached her from behind. "Maybe I could even do a bit of discreet canoodling before I confess my undying love for another." The long, blonde hair he was currently feasting his eyes on seemed to be melting his strict moral standpoint quicker than a hot day melts a child's ice cream. He bent down and clasped his hands over Mandy's eyes and whispered in her ear, "Guess who, my lovely little librarian?"

True Crimes USA was a slender volume, measuring no more than half an inch in thickness, in sharp contradistinction to the hardback version of 'The Complete Works of William Shakespeare' which lay next to it on the library table. Here was a sizeable piece of work, measuring some four inches thick, and crammed full of words. Ask any young 'O' level English student who has had to sit through four hours of Hamlet at the Swan Theatre, Stratford upon Avon, and they will tell you that Shakespeare wrote lots of words, most of them unintelligible. There is a simple mathematical formula which, quoting loosely, states that loads of words equates to loads of pages, which in turn equates to loads of weight. The Complete Works of William Shakespeare was, by any definition, a weighty tome.

It was this very book that the blinded and terrified librarian now reached for. Being blessed with a vivid imagination and fearing erroneously that she had become the thirty-sixth victim of the Library Lothario, she swung the book, which was just a tad heavier than a building brick, to where she imagined her assailant's head to be, and she was not misguided in her calculation. The book caught David square on the brow, sending him reeling backwards.

The librarian swung round just in time to see him circling unsteadily, clutching his face and trying to decide on a comfortable spot to collapse onto, like a stricken boxer just seconds before the man in the short-sleeved white shirt starts wagging his index finger and counting up to ten. Seizing her moment, Mandy shoved David heavily, sending him flying into a small storeroom. Thinking quickly, she slammed the door shut and turned the key. She then ran into the office to phone the police.

David Day, only two minutes previously the dashing young hero who dispensed sweet nothings into the ear of a woman who plainly adored him, was now David Dazed, with a knob the size of a duck egg spoiling the elegant line of his brow, his vision blurred, his mind befuddled. It had all happened so quickly that he still didn't have the foggiest notion as to why he was in yet another store cupboard against his will. Were there two mad people currently doing the rounds in Kinver? Perhaps they were a husband and wife gang, and the husband would be in shortly to expose himself. The next burning question to ponder was what had happened to his head? All he could remember was a bright flash, and then pandemonium and agony.

Surveying the room as best he could, he noticed a small window just above a book shelf, though currently it resembled two overlapping windows that were made of jelly. As his focus slowly returned, he could see a latch, which thankfully was unlocked. Outside the door, female voices were getting hysterical, and he had no desire to hang around for another vicious beating with what he now reckoned must have been a cricket bat. The window was a tight fit, but a brief reconnaissance mission revealed a grassy bank or knoll on the other side, and given the stark choice between another belting at the hands of some mad librarian and a broken ankle caused by leaping ten feet through a small window, he chose the latter.

The big problem, however, was not the actual jump. It was the fact that he would have to enter the window cavity headfirst, which then, logically speaking, meant his dive to earth would also be headfirst, unless he could manage a triple somersault with toe-loop on the way down, and thereby also impress any passing Swedish Olympic judges.

David, after careful thought, didn't feel that this was within his athletic capabilities, and, having a vivid imagination to equal Mandy's, could see himself landing heavily on his hands, which would have certainly resulted in broken wrists, and both arms being shunted deep into his chest cavity and out the other end. A savage beating was now looking ever more favourable. Then he began to rethink his exit strategy. By going out headfirst with his bottom resting on the window-ledge, his head would emerge facing the outer library wall. All he had to do them was grab hold of the guttering just above the window, pull himself out, and drop onto his feet. Admittedly he still risked a pair of broken ankles, but even in his foggy mental state, David realized that he earned a living with his hands, not his feet.

All went reasonably well until the final thrust to clear the window frame. He had forgotten to include in his calculations, the spike of the brass window catch, which became entangled in the belt loop his trousers. As David launched himself into space with incredible gusto, the catch held on to his flimsy leg wear, tearing them to shreds in the process, and it was a completely trouserless and severely winded young man that hit the grassy bank heavily seconds later.

Those Doubting Thomas's who are already holding their hands aloft and protesting that trousers do not simply disintegrate at the sight of a small brass spike should assess the facts of the case, and hear all the evidence before jumping to conclusions.

Take firstly, members of the jury, the case of John Gough, a powerfully-built footballer that David had been at Tipperton Grammar School with. During one extremely well-attended and important house match, he had executed a sliding tackle in the hope of depriving the agile and gazelle-like Danny Sims of the ball, only to get back on his feet seconds later devoid of all semblance of shorts. The muscles in his huge legs had all expanded in unison, tested the stitches on his skin-tight leg-wear and found them wanting. The shorts lay beside him on the pitch in two neat halves, leaving him dangerously exposed, especially as he had omitted to wear any form of undergarment.

David had tried, on numerous occasions, to blank out the memory of John Gough, as he walked the gauntlet back to the dressing room, past hundreds of hysterical pupils of both sexes, but the memory was having none of it. It was there for life. David's trouser loss was, however, different in many respects. That day he had been wearing a pair of old and flimsy cotton Oxford bags, which were far too big for him around the waist and held together with a red and green elasticated snake belt. Being the size of a stick insect around the middle and a gangly six-feet tall, this presented problems when purchasing leg wear. It was either correct for his waist, but six inches short in the leg, or correct for the leg, but big enough to accommodate close friends around the waist. When the brass spike took hold of his trousers, David simply fell out of them, shoes and all, with an action not too dissimilar to that of emptying a small goldfish out of a plastic bucket. There was, however, one aspect of John Gough's situation that *was* similar to David's. Neither of them had been wearing underpants.

As he lay, dazed and confused on the bank, staring back up at the window where his Oxford bags hung, blowing in the breeze like a pair of flags, he suddenly became cognizant of this same breeze blowing gently across his genitalia, a sensation that ordinarily he would have savoured. Now though, wasn't the right time. He struggled to his feet and pulled his cheesecloth shirt down over the offending articles. As he rose, so the pounding increased within his head. The bank behind the library was quiet and unpopulated, but he knew that he would have to traverse the busy high street in order to catch the bus back to the castle.

Catch the bus? What on earth was he thinking? How could he jump on a bus without his trousers, or even pay for the bus ride, for that matter? There was no option. He would have to hit the High Street at fifty miles per hour, hoping that everyone was looking the other way at the time, and then escape down the side of the butcher's shop, through the gardens, across the stream and into the farmer's fields. The short way back to Stanmore Castle.

Taking a deep breath and hanging on for dear life to his shirt tails, David sped off like a demented whippet, slaloming this way and that through the busy street. Shoppers stared in blank disbelief as this stick-like individual pelted past them with legs like knotted white string in baseball boots. A lady sipping coffee in the café took some the wrong way and had to be forcibly slapped on the back by her friend. Others shouted, "It's him! The one we've been warned about!"

The police car that was surging through the High Street en-route to an emergency call from the library paused briefly, not knowing which incident to pursue, but fortunately for David, opted for the crazed madman in the library, rather than the semi-naked madman in the street. If only they had realised that the two were actually one and the same.

There wasn't far to go now. He could see the butcher's shop just yards away, and after that he would be observed only by passing sheep. It was then that the rusty pliers took hold of his exposed genitals and he fell to the floor, screaming in agony. For a man who was supposedly too delicate to drive a car, he was testing his body to the limits. His operation scar was throbbing, and the testicle fluid was back with a vengeance.

It is hard to describe accurately the effect that such a spectacle was having on the good folk of Kinver. Some turned the other way, and some gawped. One middle-aged gentleman decided to confront the stricken naturist. A hand grabbed David by the scruff of his neck and hauled him up.

"What you doin'?" asked the man. On close inspection, David realized that he was wearing an American confederate army uniform. "Why you got yer li'l ol'cocky-doodle out, partner? I'm gonna have to arrest you."

There are times when a man can argue his way out of difficulty, and there are other times when all discussion is useless. David let go of his shirt tails and punched the man hard in the nose. He'd never hit another human being before, but had often fantasized about it. In his mind, he would land the punch, but there would be no strength whatsoever in it, which would cause his would-be victim to sneer briefly, before proceeding to beat him to a bloody pulp. It was almost certainly this fear of being inadequate that had prevented his pugilistic career from flourishing, rather than just his naturally pacifist nature. He needn't have worried. The village madman hit the deck and stayed there, waiting for the small, dapper man in the short-sleeved white shirt to arrive and commence the ten second count. To whip down the butcher's alleyway and disappear across country was, with David, the work of an instant. He was a sensitive soul, and knew instinctively when he wasn't wanted around.

Half an hour later, mud-stained, scratched to pieces and with the mother of all headaches, David limped into the castle, making a beeline for Julian's little office. He had no real desire to explain his erratic behaviour to his new bosses for the second time, but he was so desperate for paracetomol that he was willing to do so. Luck, for once, was on his side. Both Julian and Percy were at the Fox public house, just down the lane, celebrating their new exhibit with bangers and mash and a pint of Tutton Ale.

He crawled into the office and headed for the tiny medicine cabinet above the sink, where Julian kept a basic supply of tablets, band-aids and creams. He snatched a strip of paracetomol and swallowed two tablets with a glass of water, keeping the other two in the breast pocket of his shirt in case he needed them later.

Meanwhile, back at the library, police officers Donald and Pongo were interviewing a distraught librarian. At least, Donald was. Pongo was sitting at the table, helping himself to the chocolate digestive biscuits and reading True Crime USA.

"We still have his t-t-trousers," sobbed the still-trembling young woman. Gillian, the senior librarian, placed a comforting arm around her shoulders and urged her to sip at the strong sweet tea she had made for her.

Donald examined the trousers carefully. "There's some money in the pocket, and what's this? It feels like a credit card in the back pocket. No, it's his bus pass. Now we're getting somewhere!"

He removed the card and studied the details. His face seemed to drain of blood. "Pongo, you're not going to believe this."

He handed Pongo the card. Pongo shook his head slowly and raised his left hand to his brow, giving his bald head a scratch.

"We know this character, Miss," sighed Donald. "In fact, we go way back. We first met him walking in a torrential downpour, carrying a guitar in a cardboard box under his arm. Naturally, we were curious, and to be honest, we suspected that he might have stolen it. As it turned out, he hadn't. He was taking it home to repair it for his friend; a friend, incidentally, that he couldn't remember the name of. The second time we met up was when he'd just bought a rusty old Mini to travel to Art College in. We were given a tip-off about a Mini answering that description containing an IRA bomb, so we blew it to smithereens with a controlled explosion. I must admit, that *was* our fault. Then, lo and behold, if he doesn't crop up again, involved in a fine art forgery scam. You have to understand Miss; he's a nice lad really. It's just this knack he has of getting into unbelievable scrapes."

"I don't call unprovoked physical assault being nice, do you officer?"

"Well no, but trust me Miss, there will be some kind of misunderstanding. There always is with David. He's barmy, but not bad."

"Well I want him tracked down, officer," sobbed Mandy. "I want to hear what he has to say about this."

"Very well," agreed Donald. "Now let's just have a quick look in the storeroom again, to see if he's left any other clues for us."

Gillian, Mandy, Donald and Pongo stood in the tiny little room, examining the tattered remains of David's Oxford bags still attached to the brass spike.

"Incidentally, why are you called Pongo, officer?" asked Gillian. He coloured slightly at her enquiry.

"You may or may not find out in the fullness of time, Miss," smiled Donald cryptically, "But perhaps a small, enclosed space such as this is the best place to find out, eh Pongo? At least our David's left the window open!"

* * *

Percy and Julian returned an hour later, refreshed and eager to get to work. As they strolled through the museum en-route for Julian's office, Percy tapped his curator on the shoulder. His face registered puzzlement.

"Notice anything unusual about Elton today?"

Julian's jaw dropped. "He's got no trousers on."

"What on earth is going on around this place?" asked Percy, exasperated. "Now the exhibits are exposing themselves."

"They're not, actually," laughed Julian. "Look, he hasn't got a todger!"

Percy had a lot more he wished to say on the subject, but he was interrupted by Jethro, the young gardener, who had just arrived, leaving a trail of something unspeakable across the polished tiled floor from the bottom of his wellies.

"Excuse me Mr Payne, sir," he began. Had he been wearing a cap, he would have doffed it. "You know you arsed me to look out fer yer brother, who was coming to tow away the old caravan?"

Percy nodded and turned to Julian. "Jethro's on about the big caravan out in the courtyard. My younger brother is going to take it away, refurbish it and add a few school tables and chairs, so that we can use it as a nature study classroom for the school trips. It's so big; it can hold a group of ten kids and a teacher, no trouble."

"Good idea," agreed Julian. "It'll do till we can afford a Portakabin."

"Anyway," continued Jethro, "He came this dinner-time, while you was at the pub, and took it on the back of his Range Rover.

"Excellent!" smiled Percy. Jethro tugged at his forelock and retired to the garden.

"You see Julian," said Percy. "Things are slowly getting better. Brother is a skilled carpenter. He'll have the old van looking like new in a week or two. Incidentally, did you notice anything odd about Jethro?"

"Yes and no. His face does look different, but I can't put my finger on it."

"He's growing his hair longer, and it does nothing for his looks, in my opinion," frowned Percy, much to the amusement of Julian, who, hypocritically, it had to be said, had oft looked askance at his employer's coiffure. "And either I'm a Dutchman, or he's plucking his eyebrows."

Feeling there was not much he could add to this one way or the other, Julian continued down the corridor to his den.

"Have you been in here, Percy?" he asked.

"No, why?"

"Well, I hope the madman hasn't broken in again. First Elton's trousers are gone, and now my door is open, and I distinctly remember it being closed when we left for the pub. If those ashabtis are missing, we're in the shit!"

They entered the office, where the ashabtis sat staring at them from the old shoebox.

"Thank Christ for that!" said Julian, breathing a sigh of relief. "But someone *has* been in here. My petty cash tin's been raided, the medicine cabinet is open, and I never leave it open. And look! Someone has taken my sleeping pills."

## CHAPTER 5

### The Curse of Tutton Common

David desperately needed to go home and get some rest. His head was really hurting now, and the paracetamol, which usually worked very quickly, didn't seem to have been the least bit effective. Maybe his wound was too serious for a couple of tablets to be of use, and he really needed to be hospitalized. He had heard about the dangers of concussion, and knew that the main symptoms were an overwhelming desire to sleep, coupled with delirium. Suddenly, he felt very frightened, as he chugged home on the top deck of the Kinver to Stourbridge bus, fighting the sea of tiredness that was engulfing him. He realized that his fiancée was not at home to look after him, and his parent's house was too far away. He could slip into a coma and die, and no one would be any the wiser. Suzanne would return from her parents' a week later and find him decomposing in the kitchen. It was not a nice thought.

The bus driver was not helping matters either, by bouncing over every pothole and 'sleeping policeman' he could. The gentle rocking sensation was accelerating David's descent into the abyss, coupled with the fact that he had consumed not one powerful sleeping pill, which was the stated dose, but two. Quite soon he had only one eye open at a time, like a late-night reader struggling to complete his final chapter. He licked his finger and wet his lashes, but it was no use. His weary head slumped forwards, and he was gone.

* * *

David came to very slowly indeed. He was freezing cold and felt paralysed, as if some unseen pigmy hunter had blown a poisoned dart into the back of his head. The room was dark and grainy, with the vague silhouettes of furniture looming out of the fog. He tried to rise, but his legs gave way and he slumped back down again. 'Look on the bright side', his befuddled brain argued. He was still alive, and not decomposing. His next attempt at standing was more successful, and with the aid of a chair back, he was able to get to his feet. He staggered forwards, grabbing another chair for support. There were, he mused, a lot of chairs in the room, and as he made his way forwards, he realized that they were neatly positioned in two rows, with an aisle down the middle.

Could it really be that he was still on the bus, and if so, where the hell was it? David's eyes gradually adjusted to the light, and he was able to clamber down the spiral staircase to the driver's cabin. The front doors would not budge, but he had often travelled on buses, and remembered a large red button that the driver pressed to open them. He reached over, located the button and the doors sprung open. Mightily relieved, he limped off the bus and made his way to the terminus doors which were locked. The driver had obviously looked briefly upstairs through his mirror and seen no one. It was hardly surprising. When David awoke he had been slumped behind the seat in a ball, and now he was paying for that poor sleeping posture with an awful stiff neck to go with his headache.

Next to the main doors was a large filthy window, which thankfully let in sufficient light for him to estimate that it was very early morning, and the vibrant clamour of the dawn chorus confirmed this. He'd obviously been asleep in the terminus all night, but the burning question was, which terminus? Not for the first time that day, David prepared to escape through a window. He found a large spanner from a nearby work bench and hurled it through the glass. Quickly knocking out the various shards that remained intact, he placed an old oily carpet over the window frame and gingerly crawled through the space, hoping and praying that, for once, God would spare him an impromptu pliers attack, or an angry bus depot manager with a big stick. Luckily, neither materialized, and David meandered towards the outside world in a stupor, looking for clues.

He didn't have to look far. He was in the vicinity of New Street Railway Station, Birmingham, a place he knew well. Still fighting an overwhelming urge to curl up and sleep, he found his way to the platforms, and asked a jolly-looking West Indian gentleman in a grimy-collared uniform where he could find the train for Stourbridge.

"Platform tree," he replied, consulting his crib notes, "but 'urry up man. It am goin' soon."

David summoned up his last iota of strength and ran to platform three, his tired eyes drifting in and out of focus. He opened a door and leapt onto the train, just as it began to pull slowly out of the station. He crawled through a couple of full carriages, until he finally came across a carriage that was completely empty. The pain in his head was becoming unbearable now, and he was exhausted and hungry. The previous occupant of his seat had left the Observer, a half bottle of still mineral water and three quarters of a sausage roll. He glanced under the table at his ridiculous corduroy trousers, which were at least eight inches too short and filthy. He looked like a beggar, and beggars could not be choosers, so he grabbed the sausage roll and wolfed it down. He then took out the last two paracetomol tablets and swallowed them with a swig of mineral water. It was a half hour trip back to Stourbridge, give or take. He picked up the Observer and decided to improve his mind. Twelve words later, he was unconscious.

"Wakey wakey!" The ticket inspector gently nudged David, so as not to startle him. "We're at the station son. Time to get up." David opened one eye. His headache had subsided a little and he didn't feel quite as comatose. He opened the other eye. "Are we here?"

"Yes son. I should really have clipped your ticket, but you were spark out. Have you been in a fight? Maybe had a few too many perhaps? It's often the way round here. Look, I'm not judgmental. I was young once, son, but be careful. You look like you could do with a wee bath too."

"Where are we?" asked David.

"Glasgow Central, son. Last stop."

"What? You're joking!"

"I never joke about train destinations, son. Glasgow Central it is."

"But I caught the Stourbridge train from platform three."

"No you didn't, son. You may have to get your wee eyes tested. We left from platform eight."

"Oh, Jesus Christ! This is a disaster."

David left the train with no luggage, the ill-fitting clothing he stood up in, and approximately one pound thirty-eight pence in his pocket. Robinson Crusoe would probably have looked about the same after his first month on the island. The only real difference was that David, so far, didn't have a huge beard.

Totally disorientated, he staggered around the platform, not really knowing what to do next. One pound thirty-eight wouldn't get him back to Stourbridge, and it certainly wouldn't find him board and lodgings in Glasgow. He was between a rock and a hard place. He didn't even have any artist's materials. At least then he could have caricatured his way home, something he'd often fantasized about trying. The contents of Julian's petty cash tin wouldn't even get him a decent meal.

All around him he could hear unfamiliar, broad Scottish accents; people greeting old friends, hugging grandmothers, returning to or leaving for colleges, kissing, cuddling, smoking and swearing. Glasgow life was in full swing, and for the first time in his life, David understood what it felt like to be lonely, unwanted and unloved. All of a sudden, he was eleven years old again and lost in the fog halfway up Brierley Bank High Street, crying for his mother.

A voice very close to his right ear spoke softly.

"Yo aw-right, ode pal?"

David was hardly Hercule Poirot, but he could detect the origins of an accent when he heard one.

"Oh yes, thanks. I'm in a spot of bother though. I've been ill, and I slept from Brum to Glasgow. The trouble is, I was supposed to be heading for Stourbridge."

"Bloody 'ell! Yo took the scenic route day yer?"

"'Fraid so. My family are going to be worried sick. I've got no money and I'm lost."

The good-natured Brummie eyed David up and down. He seemed an honest enough lad, but it didn't seem a good idea to be lending him cash to buy a train ticket home. He didn't have a lot spare anyway, and he might never see it again.

"I'll tell yer what," said the Brummie. "I've come to climb Ben Nevis with a pal of mine. He's been up here at university studying engineering. It's summat I've always fancied doing - don't ask me why! Me mate's meeting me here soon and driving us up to Fort William. We'll climb the mountain, subject to good weather, stay overnight, and then he's driving down to the Midlands to see his folks. If yo'm really stuck, yo can hitch a ride with us, but either yo'll have to climb Ben Nevis tomorrah or else yo'll have to amuse yerself for a day while we do. What yer reckon?"

David had never had homosexual tendencies, but he could cheerfully have kissed the man at that point. "Thank you.

Thank you. I can give you one pound thirty-eight petrol money."

"Keep yer money in yer pocket, ode pal," smiled the Brummie. "Yo might need it tomorrah."

* * *

Julian was worried. David had gone down the library before lunch the day before, and he still hadn't returned. He'd phoned his house several times but there was no reply. Then there was the ongoing mystery of Elton's trousers, the sleeping pills and the missing petty cash. As mysteries went, this was a strange one. It should have been a good day, what with the fascinating new discoveries, but the young curator was troubled. He'd posted the black and white photo and a couple of decent Polaroids of the ashabtis for Adrian to study, and was delighted to hear from his brother's secretary that they'd arrived safely. She had promised him that her boss would be phoning back that morning with his preliminary findings, with a more detailed report to follow as soon as possible. Now, all this was over-shadowed by David's disappearance.

The door burst open, and Percy entered. He was upright for a change, but looking flustered. "The travellers have stolen my caravan," he snarled, kicking the wastepaper basket into the air.

"What?"

"Do you remember Jethro telling us that my younger brother had arrived and towed the caravan away? Well, I just phoned him to ask how it was progressing, and he said that he couldn't pick it up till Friday, as he'd been a bit busy. Can you believe the cheek of the bastards? They just breezed in and hitched it up. They even waved at Jethro, and he waved back, the gormless turd."

Julian sighed a heavy sigh. "When sorrows come, they come not in single spies but in battalions. David's disappeared. You don't think he's had enough of this place and done a runner do you?"

"Currently, I wouldn't blame him," moaned Percy, head in hands. "Perhaps his hernia's come undone and he's in hospital. Have you checked there?"

Julian thought this was a possibility and reached for the phone, just as it rang. He answered it. It was his brother, Adrian, with his initial findings. Percy pulled his chair closer to the phone with childish excitement.

"Hi Jools!" chirruped the professor. "Have I got news for you! Pin back your ears and take notes. I've had the boffins on this. Firstly though, a bit of background. As you know, Howard Carter discovered the tomb of Tutankhamun on November the twenty-sixth, nineteen-twenty-two, whilst in the pay of Lord Carnarvon, and this was the greatest find ever, so obviously it overshadowed everything else. Nefertiti, who was the wife of the Pharaoh Akhenaten, and a powerful lady in her own right, has not to this day been found, though a lot has been discovered about her, including the famous limestone sculpture in all the text books. Now her father was a bloke called Ay, who became Pharaoh after King Tut, and may even have had a hand in bumping old Tut off. Your Lord Hickman was out there at the same time as Carter, and he discovered the infinitely more modest tomb of Rametup, husband of Sippahottut and hairdresser to Nefertiti - yes, I did say hairdresser, hence, I presume, the comb. Hickman cleaned out the tomb and sneaked his treasures back to England, much to the disgust of the Egyptian government, who quite rightly felt as if they had been robbed of all their best stuff by English upper-crust toffs. Our research shows that this Hickman, whilst not a major figure, did very well out of it all and amassed a small fortune in relics. Round about nineteen twenty-three he disappeared without trace and his castle eventually fell to his son, who carried on the line, once his many debtors had carted away most of the oil paintings and furniture. Now, here's the spooky bit. Our hieroglyphics bod, Professor Anton Porter, has deciphered the words on the black and white photo and on the relics for you. Can I ask, are you superstitious, brother?"

“Not at all, as you well know.”

“Then I’ll continue. The wording on the wall is from the tomb of Rametup and indicates that there is a curse, just as there was with Tutankhamun. It states that anyone desecrating the tomb will crumble to dust and disappear from the earth, roughly translated. The writing on the wooden comb says; ‘Here is the comb of Rametup, used on none but Queen Nefertiti. A curse shall fall on any that use the comb, other than her.’ After that, it goes on about crumbling to dust and disappearing off the face of the earth again, which seems to be the punishment of choice for these ancient Egyptian types. Now here’s the creepy, final sentence. It says that Rametup will rise from the dead to avenge those who desecrate his final resting place, and they will also be cursed with fire, plagues and pestilence, etcetera. I wouldn’t worry too much about that. I think it’s one of those standard clauses they put in to deter the grave robbers.”

Julian appeared to have suffered a minor stroke, and was not responding.

“Was that enough information for you Jools? You’ve gone quiet!”

“Oh, erm, yes. Thank you ever so much, Ade,” replied Julian, stunned to the core. “Look, I’ll phone you back. Something rather important’s come up.”

Julian dialled the local hospital with trembling fingers, but it was as he suspected. David had not been admitted. He called David’s parents, and casually enquired as to his whereabouts, without giving too much away. There was no point in worrying them to death at this stage. Predictably, they told Julian to ring David’s new little semi-detached house in Stourbridge, that he was buying with his fiancée, Suzanne. The curator replaced the receiver and ruffled his hair, sending pencil stubs tinkling to the floor.

“Percy, this is serious - cue the creepy music. Old Lord Hickman discovered Rametup’s tomb, and soon after disappeared off the face of the earth, together with his wife and butler - everyone who’d seen and touched the treasures, in other words. Now you discover these bloody ashabtis and the comb in the attic, and David disappears without trace. It’s no coincidence, man. David brushed that comb through his hair. I didn’t, and you didn’t. That is a fact. My hair’s never seen a comb in its life, and I’m glad about that now.”

“And you are the one who’s not superstitious?” queried Percy. “Look old son. Relax! David has probably got himself embroiled in one of his situations again; you know what he’s like. He’ll no doubt be here tomorrow, keen to get on with it, like nothing’s happened, you mark my words. I bet he’s just a bit under the weather because of his hernia operation. They say it takes weeks before you’re really up to scratch. I’ll bet you a fiver he’s at home, fast asleep as we speak.”

“I hope so,” frowned Julian. “Anyway, let’s lighten the tone, eh? Has that librarian sent you her samples yet? It’s taking long enough.”

“No, not a sausage. Disappointing really, she seemed so keen. Look, I have a few chores to attend to. I have to go and see the village bobbies about the stolen caravan, and while I’m down there, I’ll look in on Gillian and see what’s keeping her, and maybe call over to Dave’s place, just to put your mind at rest. And cheer up, old son. We have three great new exhibits for the museum. Draft a press release and let’s get those punters through the doors, eh?”

Percy disappeared down the corridor, leaving Julian alone with his thoughts. There was nothing he could do to about David for the time being, so he tried to shut out all the unpleasant images of mummy resurrections and decided to apply his nose to the grindstone. There was a hell of a lot of work to do, so he resolved to work late and clear the decks. Hard work had always made him feel better when he was feeling stressed, and he currently didn't have a nice lady friend to go home to anyway, so he resolved get on with it and burn the midnight oil.

Julian, a native of Oxfordshire, had relocated to Tutton when he landed his job at the Museum of Local Life. He'd initially rented a small village-centre cottage, but Percy had offered him the recently renovated old vineyard offices within the grounds of the castle at a fraction of the cost, and Julian had snatched his hand off. The only trouble with this cosy arrangement was that he was living and working at the castle, and often, after a mentally tiring day in the museum, he was too exhausted to drive down to the village in search of soul-mates. He was also too tired to cook proper meals, and relied on the nearby Fox Inn, or T.V. dinners. After a particularly bad day, when even the thought of using the microwave was all too much, he had even been known to suck them frozen.

The next time Julian glanced at his wall clock, it was nine p.m., and he was starving. He'd worked straight through his lunch break, and onwards into the night, totally engrossed in his work. When he first arrived, it was hard to rake up any enthusiasm for Tarbuck and friends, or the Butterflies and Moths collection, but now they had real, important relics to display, and he felt that these were but the springboard for higher things. He was determined to turn this hole in the ground into one of the premier tourist attractions in the West Midlands, even if it killed him.

Enough was enough though. His addled mind was no longer fit to type press releases, and he needed sustenance. Percy, his usual companion come opening time, had popped back at teatime and declared that he was going round his brother's place, so tonight Julian was on his own. There was a frozen block of fish fingers in the freezer. He could boil up a few peas in five minutes and see if the croquette potatoes were still in date. Most of the wholemeal bread was still mould-free, and there was a bottle of Blue Nun in the rack. Things didn't get much better than that. It was time to call it a day and stagger across the courtyard to the old stable block. He rose unsteadily, his knees creaking like those of an old man. He had always been troubled by creaking joints, thanks to his sedentary work and a general loathing of exercise. However, this particular night, they curiously continued to creak, long after he had stood up. Then he realized that the noise was no longer emanating from his legs, but from his door. A chill raced through Julian's body as his over-active mind went into overdrive. The hairs stood up on the back of his neck as he watched the door slowly opening into the room.

Hitlerina came sidling in, wrapping her elegant form around Julian's corduroy-clad legs. She dropped one of her little presents at the curator's feet.

It was a severed human finger.

# CHAPTER 6

## Highland Games

The Brummie and his mate waved goodbye to David at the foothills of Ben Nevis, and promised to meet up with him that evening at seven, when hopefully they would have completed their challenge in one piece. After a terrible, freezing cold, sleepless night in a cramped transit van, still pungent from the deadly cocktail of bodily gasses released as the inmates slept, David was quite looking forward to some time on his own. The Brummie, ever courteous, had asked their young travelling companion if he cared to join them on the climb, but David explained that he was medically exempt. He called after them to break a leg, quickly realizing that, whilst this may have been the correct term of encouragement for actors, it was less than diplomatic for mountaineers.

Now he had around eight hours to waste, which was difficult with the changeable weather, the lack of transport and one pound thirty-eight pence. First priority was to get to a call box and let everyone know that he was safe, if a little off course, so he walked back down the track and onto the main road. He knew that the van had travelled a short distance from a largish town of sorts, but he couldn't remember what it was called, and as he'd been travelling in a converted transit van with no rear windows, it was difficult to see precisely where he was going. The road sign said that Fort William was left, and Inverness was right. David tossed a coin and decided on Inverness. There was bound to be a call box somewhere along the main road. This, after all, was a civilized and extraordinarily beautiful country.

After an hour's hike with no phone box to be found anywhere, David's groin was aching, and threatening to unzip at any moment. He sat down in the grass verge, and rested his back against a large concrete street lamp, frustrated and starving. He had seen several expensive-looking pubs and restaurants, but the money he had was not sufficient to buy a starter, let alone a dinner, and he looked far too scruffy to be admitted, even if it was. He had already noticed fellow walkers crossing the road when they caught sight of him, which was distressing. He still couldn't make up his mind whether this was through fear of being mugged, or just the smell.

As he sat, forlorn and close to tears, a man with a bright red face and a huge, pock-marked purple nose approached him, riding an ancient bicycle in a very unsteady fashion. David dragged himself off the ground and clung onto the street lamp, fascinated to see how long this obviously intoxicated local character could stay upright, given that he had just meandered into the path of an oncoming juggernaut, causing the petrified driver to blast his mighty horn in protest.

"Ah, fek ye, ye bastard!" screamed the drunk, waving both his fists in the air. This, unfortunately, proved to be his undoing. There are cyclists who can ride without hands. One sees them regularly in the coverage of such events as the Tour de France. This particular cyclist, however, could not. The rusty bicycle careered sharply towards David, causing him to take swift evasive action. Unfortunately, what stood next to David was what is known in scientific terms as the immovable object. Jimmy McGregor, to give this sozzled character a convenient pseudonym, hit the lamppost head on, catapulting him into the hedgerow with a terrible force. The rusty bicycle parted company with its owner, halfway into a spirited, if slightly incoherent rendition of 'Loch Lomond, with its eerily prophetic lyrics, and was promptly flattened by a passing Landrover.

David ran over to examine the cyclist, who was currently having a deep and meaningless conversation with the hedgerow.

"Are you okay, mate?" he asked, somewhat predictably.

"I love ye," replied the man, touchingly.

David dragged him out of the prickly hedge and sat him down.

"You saved ma life, pal," continued the drunk. "I'd like to buy ye a wee drink."

David thanked him, but insisted that it was a little early at nine-fifteen a.m., and besides, there were no pubs to be seen.

"I'm afraid your bike's wrecked," he continued, taking a step backwards after experiencing the first waft of the man's breath.

"Och, it doesn'ae matter pal," insisted the drunk. "I stole it anyway."

He then lay down in the grass and suspended the interview at nine-seventeen precisely. David walked over to the road and removed the bike, before another vehicle could run over it. The back end was, in fairness, not too bad, but the front wheel was severely buckled. A quick search in the saddle bag revealed a cyclist's multi-spanner, so, having nothing better to do, he removed the damaged wheel.

David was a keen cyclist, and as a child had often repaired his cycle speedway bikes in the back yard. Occasionally he had had to straighten wheels buckled in racing accidents, but none were as bad as this one. Using the concrete lamp post as a lever, he straightened the wheel as best he could, and after a few intuitive kicks in the right spots, it was, if one viewed it from a mile away through scratched sunglasses, sort of roundish again. He fitted the wheel into the front forks and tried to spin it. It was catching badly on the brakes, but David estimated that if they were removed, it was feasible that the mangled wreck might work, at least for a time. Using the same combination spanner, he quickly took off the front brake mechanism and tried again.

Voila! It would never win a Tour de France, but a circus clown would probably be able to ride it for a few yards. Now the poor chap could at least complete his journey home, once he'd sobered up. David, for all his faults, was a caring and thoughtful young man; his mother and father had bought him up that way. However, there did exist, lurking within him, a Machiavellian streak that surfaced in times of desperation. He needed transport urgently, whilst the drunk just needed a nap. He was miles from home and desperate. The drunk probably lived a mile down the road. The drunk had stolen the bike in the first place. David, after all, could argue that he was merely doing his civic duty by trying to return it to its rightful owner, once he'd had a bit of use out of it himself. Moral discussion over, he mounted the bike and rattled erratically down the road, desperately trying to avoid juggernauts. After five or so precarious minutes in the saddle, he spotted a red phone box and brought his rusting steed to a grinding halt which saw most of the ball bearings in the front wheel hub make a daring dash for the open spaces. He opened the door and went in, but was dismayed to see that vandals had smashed the telephone receiver to pieces, and sprayed 'M.U.F.C.' all over the windows.

He slumped out of the phone box and looked to the heavens, which were looking black and ominous, their custom in the Highlands. Calling out to no one in particular, he wailed, "They have landed a man on the moon. They have cured most of the terrible diseases, and invented computers. Surely, it is not beyond the wit of man for someone to invent a little phone that we can carry around in out bloody pockets, for f***'s sake!"

He sat on the grass verge and cried unmanly tears. He had finally reached his lowest ebb. He was tired, hungry, afraid and lonely, and he wanted a cuddle from his Suzanne.

Then the heavens opened.

Scrambling onto the stricken bicycle, he began to pedal like fury to try and escape the torrential rain. This wasn't the feeble Sassenach-type shower that David was used to, and within seconds, he was as wet as a human being could get. He turned off the busy main road to decrease his chances of being flattened by a truck and headed for a sign saying 'Caledonian Canal – Neptune's Ladder'. Another, smaller sign promised teas, coffees and toasted snacks at the lock-side café, and it was this potential haven that he was striving to reach when disaster struck.

The dismantling of the front brake had not worried an experienced rider like David unduly. He knew that bicycles were also fitted with rear brakes as standard, and either would suffice, should push come to shove, though admittedly, they didn't work awfully well in wet conditions. What he hadn't catered for, however, was the possibility of a rear brake malfunction, caused by a total absence of rubber brake pads. As he approached Neptune's Ladder, (a great staircase of locks designed to gradually drop boats to a lower level of canal, as they proceeded towards the upper Highlands and the West Coast) he realized that, unless he took evasive action, he would join the rather grand-looking vessel currently availing itself of the facilities.

He squeezed both brake levers instinctively, quickly realizing that half of the double act was lying in a ditch next to a sleeping drunk. He then squeezed the remaining brake with twice the intensity, as if to redress the balance, but was dismayed to hear not the reassuring sound of rubber on rim, but the disconcerting banshee-like wail of bare metal on bare metal, accompanied by a rather wonderful display of sparks. Spectacular though it undoubtedly was, as a device designed to save its rider from hurtling headfirst into a canal, it was woefully inadequate, and there was a terrible inevitability about what came next.

Tipperton Grammar School had its own swimming baths and provided once-a-week swimming lessons for its charges. During David's six year sentence, these lessons were sandwiched between geography and maths, the teachers of which were renowned for their insistence on punctuality and iron discipline. This gave the pupils precisely forty minutes to leave the geography classroom, run over to the changing rooms, leap in the water, fool around, dry off, get changed and hare across to the other side of the school in time for maths. David, who never particularly enjoyed getting his hair wet, chose not to bother.

Precisely two seconds before his rusty bicycle left terra firma, lemming-like, and headed for the waters below, he began to seriously regret that decision. At the age of twenty-four, he still had no inkling of how to swim. He was more than a little relieved, therefore, when he emerged, coughing and spluttering in the freezing cold water after his initial dunking, to find a bright orange lifebelt waiting for him. Seconds later, he was dragged onto the ocean-going cruiser and laid out on the deck, like a floundering fish.

"Are ye okay, son?" asked Gordon Young, skipper of the boat, a grey haired, bearded, fifty-something with a broad Scottish accent. "I was rather hoping I'd no have to gi' ye the kiss o' life. No offence, but ye're no ma type."

David stared blankly at the broad, cheeky face peering down at him. Behind his rescuer, he could also see a blue sky re-emerging from behind the rain clouds. This country was certainly changeable.

"I'm wet, and hungry and tired and pissed off," gurgled David. "Four emotions for the price of one - I know you Scottish folk love a bargain!"

"Och aye!" smiled Gordon. "That we do. It's nice to see ye've still a sense of humour, son. Mind you, you look like ye were well overdue for a wee bath."

"Bloody hell!" said David, sitting up with some effort. "So Scotsmen really do say 'Och aye'. Well I never."

"That we do lad," replied Gordon. "Are you ready for the bad news now? I couldn'ae save yer old bike."

"Good!" said David, standing up unsteadily. "It was a death trap."

The rain had now ceased, and the blue skies began to break through once more. Gordon asked David how he'd got himself into such a poor state, when his accent suggested an educated and reasonably articulate young man. Suddenly David realized how important appearance was, and how easy it was to label someone because of their apparel. Until now, people had always automatically placed him in a certain social standing, and now he was scoring well into the red on the class-ometer. He felt a full and detailed explanation was in order, as he had been twice written off as a down-and-out already, and he'd only been in Scotland for two days.

Gordon introduced him to Alan and Hamish who were crewing the boat, and suggested that he should clean himself up and get some food inside him before they listened to his life story. He was led down below to the generously appointed cabins, shown the shower room and handed warm towels and a change of clothes. As he groaned with ecstasy under the wonderful hot water, David pondered on the importance of hospitality and humanity, coming to the conclusion that the Scottish Highlanders had the stuff in sackfuls, unlike some of the aloof and snooty southerners he'd met. He felt grateful that he hadn't fallen in next to a boat from Chelsea. They'd have surely ignored him and carried on nibbling their canapés.

Feeling squeaky clean but a little drained from his traumatic few hours, David joined his hosts on deck.

"Would ye like a wee dram, to warm yer insides?" asked Gordon, pouring himself yet another. These Celtic sailors seemed to favour the flexible yard-arm when it came to alcohol.

"It's only a quarter to eleven. A bit early for me," replied David, and showing the iron will that had become his trade mark, took a glass. Gordon moored the boat just past the last lock and his crew began to prepare the barbecue.

"We'll eat now, son, and then you can tell us your story. Are ye in any kind of rush?"

"Not at all!" smiled David, who had never tried whisky before, but was developing a taste for it. He was a captive audience until that evening, after all, he reasoned. He could spend a leisurely hour on the boat, pop over to the café and pay for a phone call, and if need be, even walk back to Ben Nevis in time to meet his Brummie friends at seven.

He saw off his drink, only to see it filled again by Hamish. By the time the sausages and steaks were ready, David had been treated to several more, and he was feeling extremely mellow. He tried to explain to his hosts that they were possibly the kindest men he had ever met, but for some reason, he was having difficulty enunciating his words. It was probably a good idea, thought Gordon, if he went below and took a wee nap, once he'd eaten, and David was inclined to agree. He was given Hamish's cabin and told to rest for as long as he wished, and in the meantime the crew were going to get their banjos out, sing folk songs and maybe help themselves to a few more wee drams.

David was impressed with the facilities, and especially liked the gently spinning bed, a feature that he had not come across before. He sighed a contented sigh as his head hit the soft pillow, and he dissolved into sleep to the sound of 'Danny Boy'.

Meanwhile, Gordon laid down his banjo, cleared away the dinner things and prepared to set sail.

"What about the little English laddie?" asked Hamish. "He'll need to get off the boat now."

"Och, nae bother," replied Gordon. "He told me earlier that he's in nae rush. Why don't we treat him to a little cruise around the islands, eh? He looks like he could do wi' a break, bless him. He's obviously fallen on hard times, but he's a bonny lad, and I've quite taken to him."

* * *

David had only ever woken up in Scotland twice, and each time it had been a shock. The first time, he had thought he was in Stourbridge. The second time, it was the Mull of Kintyre. Perhaps, he figured, each time you went to bed, some unseen hand shifted you hundreds of miles further north. He was on deck, wearing a T shirt bearing the legend, 'See you Jimmy' and a pair of comfortable jeans. His anguished cry had prematurely halted a rendition of 'Donald, where's yer troosers?' which was possibly all for the best.

"We are *where*?"

"The Mull of Kintyre, laddie. It's a bonny place, d'ya nae think?"

"But I was meeting a Brummie near Ben Nevis at seven, to get a lift home to the Midlands!"

"Oh shit, son. We didn'ae know that. You said you were in nae rush."

"Look," said David frantically. "I thank you all for your hospitality, but you have to get me back."

"That's impossible, son," explained Gordon. "We're heading for the islands on our summer holidays. What say we ask Dougie to drop you over to the mainland in his wee fishing boat? You'll be able tae pick up a train from there and get back to Fort William."

"But I don't have any money. Even my one pound thirty-eight's lying on the bottom of the lock now. I'm completely skint!"

Gordon reached into the pocket of his shorts. "You've got an honest face, laddie. We'll hear your life story some other time. Here's twenty quid to help get ye hame. This is ma card. You can send it back to that address there. We cannae dae ony mair."

David shook their hands and thanked them profusely. Gordon escorted him onto dry land and walked over to a small fisherman's cottage on the harbour, rapping the front door sharply. A few seconds later, a small, wiry-looking man with ginger hair and a mass of freckles opened it, and smiled at the large jovial character and his companion.

"Well I never!" said Dougie. "Gordon Young. It's been a few years since ye last passed this way in yer big girly boat."

Dougie worked on a trawler, which didn't have any refinements to speak of, unlike the floating gin palace moored a few yards away.

"Dougie here went tae school with me, years ago," explained Gordon, but he prefers the company of mackerel. That's why he lives alone in this God-forsaken place, eh, Dougie?"

"The trauma of knowing you caused that," smiled Dougie. "I had to get as far away as possible."

Gordon got down to the matter in hand, sensing that David was looking uneasy and hopping from foot to foot.

"My new friend here is in a spot o' bother I'm afraid. He'll need a lift across the water to the mainland, and he'd also appreciate a phone, should ye have one."

Dougie frowned, deep in thought. "Och, nae bother, but I'm nae able to go till tomorrow, first thing. Will that do ye, son?"

David was hardly in a position to make demands. "Yes, great, if that's okay. The main thing is a phone. Can I ring home, to tell them I'm safe please?"

"Now that's where it gets more difficult," said Dougie. "I dinnae have one, son, but I can point you in the right direction. There's a call box just over there. I'm away to work now, but I'll be back this evening at seven. You can sleep in my wee box room tonight. It's nae the Ritz, but it's cosy."

Dougie gave David a spare key, and asked him not to steal anything, adding with a wink that there was bugger-all to steal anyway. He arranged to meet up that evening, and suggested a cheap eating place, if David got peckish. Gordon gave David a hug, wished him well, and reminded him that if his cheque didn't arrive within the week, he would hunt him down and mount David's testicles on a mahogany plaque in the master cabin. David replied that, given the state of them, castration was probably a good thing, and he fully intended to squander Gordon's money on whisky and prostitutes. The Scotsman climbed back aboard, and within a few minutes, the boat had chugged away into the distance, in search of the next adventure. David waved until they were just a white speck on the horizon and then walked over to the phone box.

Luckily, Manchester United's fans had not yet discovered the Mull of Kintyre, and the receiver was in good working order. After a brief detour to the Scottish Gifts Emporium to change his twenty pound note, he dialled the Museum's number. There was no one home. He dialled his parent's house - ditto. Ruby was in Brierley Bank High Street, shopping, and Len was making machine tools in Old Hill. Frustrated now, he dialled his own house, but realized that Suzanne was still away in Solihull, visiting her parents, and he didn't know their number.

He vacated the phone box and decided to try the museum later on.

* * *

Julian and Percy were having lunch in the bar of the Fox Inn, Tutton. The curator reached into his pocket and asked Percy to close his eyes and open his hand.

"How old are you?" asked Percy, eyeing his employee with a pitying look.

"Never mind, just do it!" insisted Julian. He dropped the severed human finger into Percy's hand. Percy opened his eyes, screamed, and threw the finger up into the air. It landed in an old man's pint of Tutton Ale, on the next table, which was unfortunate. Julian retrieved it, apologized, and purchased a replacement, keeping the tainted pint for himself.

"What the...." gasped Percy, shocked to the core.

"It's from Elton. Hitlerina brought it into my office yesterday. It scared the shit out of me too, at first. They're so realistic aren't they?"

Percy groaned. The museum took three steps forward, he'd pop out for a spot of lunch, and by the time he'd returned it had taken two steps back.

"I might pack this in and get a job painting the Forth Bridge," he sighed. "It might be easier."

"No news on David, I suppose?" asked Julian. "Or the caravan, or the calligraphy?"

"No. David's disappearance is really worrying me, I must admit. That pair of idiots, Laurel and Hardy - Donald and Pongo, or whatever they're called, reckon there was a sighting of the caravan heading towards Hereford, but they lost the scent. You don't think David stole the caravan do you? Maybe he was in league with an international gang, and they'd planted him at the museum to stake it out."

Julian gave him a withering look. "Of course, that's it! He's pretended to be an artist for ten years, even going to the trouble of attending a degree course in illustration, where he gained a two-one, in order that he could apply for a job at the world's most boring museum to case the joint for his traveller friends, so they could steal a caravan worth at least forty quid on the black market. It's so obvious isn't it, now you think about it!"

Percy weighed this. "So you don't think I'm barking up the right tree then?"

Julian was making a habit of looking to the heavens and sighing. He'd just done it again.

"As to Gillian," continued Percy, undeterred, "now I *can* shed a bit of light on this. I popped into the library yesterday and saw her. Evidently, she *did* drop an envelope through the letter box for me, but I told her we hadn't received it. I had another look when I got back, and I found a few scraps of soggy cream paper in the hall, which means that Bertie's eaten it as usual. She promised to knock out another one ASAP, when things have calmed down a bit. They were all a bit distracted down there, because apparently, the village madman has been at it again. Her colleague, Mandy, was attacked by him as she sat reading a book in her tea break. She whacked him with a book and locked him in a store cupboard, but when Laurel and Hardy arrived, he'd scarpered, leaving his trousers behind, together with all his money and his library card, bus pass and so on, so now they know who he is, and the boys in blue are hot on his tail. Meanwhile, out in the High Street, there was a hell of a commotion going on. They reckon the madman made a dash for freedom with his todger hanging out, and he was apprehended by this passing bloke, who was knocked unconscious for his trouble, but here's the best bit! Abbott and Costello arrive to make the arrest, and recognize the unconscious bloke as the village madman, but he's in civil war uniform and still has his trousers on. You know what this all means don't you?"

"Frankly, no."

"It means that there are two village madmen on the loose."

"Just the two?"

"Yes, but Madman Number One is dangerous. Mandy reckoned that he said he was going to rape her, strangle her and stick an ice pick in her neck."

Julian regretted having the extra pint of Tutton's that lunchtime. It seemed to be making his head swim. Feeling that he could add nothing positive to the conversation, he stood up and made his excuses. There was work to be done, exhibition stands to assemble, school bookings to be taken and fingers to glue back on. Percy decided to stick around for another quick half, and promised to look in on him later.

After much cajoling, Julian had persuaded his boss to release the funds to convert part of the old stables into a tea room, and he spent a large part of the afternoon supervising the builders. There was also a school party arriving from Dudley, and they would need to be closely scrutinized, if previous school trips were anything to go by. If and when David ever returned, and the Egyptian room was completed, they would all have to be vigilant with the exhibits. It would be disastrous if Rametup and Sippahottut were seen floating down the Staffs and Worcester canal en-route to Wales. Thank goodness his secretary, the formidable Glenda, was on hand to keep them in check, with her newly beefed-up, tattooed arms.

The day had gone reasonably well, and added a few much-needed pounds to the coffers, but Julian had had precious little time to work in his office and he was feeling frustrated. He resolved to work late for the second consecutive day that week, and clear the backlog. He hoped his employer was taking note, especially at pay review time.

He returned to his little office at just after seven, and began to get to grips with his mountain of paperwork. This was the time of day he enjoyed most, when any visitors and staff had gone home, and it was nice and quiet. After an hour of uninterrupted graft, the office door began to creak open again in its usual spooky, haunted house fashion. Julian, though still a little unnerved by the previous night's goings on, was now quite relaxed about it. He had foolishly been swept up in the tide of hysteria caused by his brother's frankly theatrical revelations about Rametup's curse. All creepy incidents, the young curator felt, had perfectly rational explanations, and from now on he was not going to be fazed by such silly tales. His theory was borne out by the appearance of Hitlerina, who seemed to need a bit of fuss at that time of night - a creature of habit if ever there was one. She sidled up to Julian's legs and criss-crossed through them, purring ecstatically as she did so. Then she dropped something at her master's feet.

It was the severed human finger again.

"Bloody hell, Hitlerina!" moaned Julian. "I've just spent ages gluing that thing back. You really are such a pain!"

He bent down to retrieve it, and let out an ear-shattering, girly shriek which sent the castle cat scurrying for cover.

This time the finger was real.

Once more, the hairs began to rise on Julian's neck. A bead of sweat formed on his nose and dripped onto the floor. Suddenly, the castle seemed very big, deserted and scary, and Julian was afraid. He had dropped the finger like a red hot potato on discovering its authenticity, and it was currently lying on his application for a council grant to help with the toilet facilities. He took one of the pencil stubs from his hair and gingerly prodded it. It was undoubtedly human, and looked withered and old, like a witch's finger. There was a hint of bone at the severed end, and some dried brown blood. Julian gulped audibly and recoiled in horror. He quickly picked up the telephone and dialled the internal line to Percy's private apartment within the castle. There was no reply. His boss had gone out to the Fox Inn, as usual. Julian sat, staring at the digit, unsure of what to do next. Suddenly, the phone rang, causing him to leap from his seat in the same manner that Highland salmon leap from streams. He snatched the receiver and formed the words, 'Hello, who's there?' but because his mouth was dry due to nerves, nothing, other than a strange gargling noise, came out. He could hear what sounded like heavy breathing at the other end.

"Who is it?" he eventually croaked. There followed a dreadful, blood-curdling scream, and then the line went dead. Julian ran as fast as his legs could carry him across the dark courtyard to his flat. He extricated his keys with trembling hand, and finally let himself in, after what seemed like an eternity of fumbling. Once inside, he slammed the door shut and slid the bolts across.

He had often seen horror films just like this on T.V. A man alone in a creepy little flat, with scores of flesh-eating zombies prowling around outside. All he needed now was some thick fog, and Julian would have the perfect cure for his constipation. In a feeble attempt to take his mind off things, he began to rummage around in the freezer for the night's meal. There were two rock-solid cod steaks of dubious vintage, around nine scraggy little bits of what were once mixed vegetables preserved in a bagful of crumbly and malodorous ice and last but least, a jubbly. Julian's dinners were often questionable, but this assortment was surely overemphasizing the bizarre note. He whistled a snatch of Mozart's Magic Flute a tad too jauntily and began to cobble together his dinner. He resolved to partake of this homage to haute cuisine in the living room, and watch a little T.V. whilst he did so, to take his mind off things.

The programme was going to have to be something very special for it to have a chance of achieving that. As he whacked the cod steak forcibly against his work surface to separate it from the other one - an operation that saw both pieces skate off across the linoleum floor in a posthumous bid to reach the open seas - Julian's mind was in turmoil. He tried to rationalize his thoughts.

1. Hitlerina had presented him with a severed finger. Fact.

2. Severed fingers have to come from bodies. Fact.

(As far as he knew, they weren't a life-form in their own right. Severed fingers didn't grow up, go to university and then get married and have babies.)

3. If there *was* a body, where was it? The finger was clearly not brand new; otherwise he wouldn't have been nearly as alarmed. A new one could have been lost by someone careless and dim, like Jethro, when he was messing with the lawn mower, whereas this finger was really withered and old, like a mummy's finger.

He swallowed a fortifying glass of Blue Nun and carried his inedible concoction into the living room, laying it down on the coffee table. The huge French windows at the far end of the room were giving him the creeps, with their view across the old vineyard. It was pleasant enough in the daylight, but now it was dark, and winged creatures of the night crawled across the outside of the windows, attracted by the light and desperate to find a way in. He walked over to them and drew the heavy draylon curtains. He was just on his way back to the soggy, microwaved lump of cod and its foul accompaniments, when he heard a faint tapping noise emanating from the very windows he had just walked away from. He sat down and picked up his knife and fork.

The tapping noise began again. Perhaps it was the insects - a particularly fat moth maybe. He forked the first rancid chunk into his mouth and grimaced. There was the noise again. It was too loud for a fat moth. He was now convinced that it was a hedgehog, lured by the smell of fish. Did hedgehogs like fish, he wondered? Certainly no one had come right out and said they definitely didn't. Maybe it was just lured to the window by the sight of all those fat moths. That was probably it! The noise began again, but this time it sounded less like a tap, and more like a dull, dragging sound. With his poor overworked neck hairs rising up and down like a fiddler's elbow, Julian picked up his plate and tiptoed over to the window, placing his ear against the curtains. The noise had stopped now. He pulled the drawstring and the curtains began to part. What he saw caused him to leap backwards in horror, sending the plateful of food crashing over the floor. He tried to scream, in order to somehow relieve the tension, but no noise would come.

There, staring him in the face, inches away behind the glass and set against a pitch black night, was an Egyptian mummy with wild, staring, evil eyes.

The human body can only take so much punishment, and then it shuts down in order to try and protect itself. Julian's was no exception. He tried to step back and run, but all of a sudden, the room began to swim. He slumped to his knees and fainted, banging his head on the television as he dropped.

# CHAPTER 7

## Donald, Whaur's Yer Troosers?

David pushed his way out of the phone kiosk and sat down on the grass verge. He'd finally succeeded in contacting Julian, only to be incapacitated by a particularly vicious attack of the testicle pliers. Once he'd got his breath back and pressed the wadding against his groin for five minutes, as instructed by Doctor Frith, (a sight that caused a suspicious old lady and her grandchild to cross the road) he re-entered the kiosk and tried again. Predictably, there was now no answer.

Other than this ongoing telephone nuisance, and the pain in the testicles, he had had rather a nice day, looking around the harbour, drinking tea and eating toast in the cute little café, chatting to locals and watching the fishing boats come and go. The time had gone very quickly, and he could now return to the cottage and await Dougie's return. He didn't have very long to wait. Dougie arrived, tired and smelly from the trawler boat, and repaired upstairs to clean himself up. He came downstairs half an hour later, resplendent in a McDonald kilt and white T shirt.

"What d'ye think? No bad, eh?" He gave David a twirl and threw a carrier bag at him. David looked inside, and pulled out another McDonald kilt.

"That's yours," smiled Dougie. "It's an unwritten law here. You have tae wear the kilt. Go and put it on."

David smiled and wrinkled up his nose, as if to insinuate that his host was pulling his leg, but Dougie appeared deadly serious. Not wishing to offend or break with tradition, he slipped upstairs and came down a few minutes later, his weedy white excuses for legs dangling beneath an oversized kilt.

"Och, that's better, David." Dougie looked his guest over with an even stare. "Now how about supper? I can cook us some fash an' chaps, and there's a decent bottle of whisky in the cupboard."

Two hours later, pleasantly full and woozy on whisky, David stood in the tiny cramped kitchen drying up, while his host washed the dishes, a perfect scene of cosy domesticity, in a cottage where no one wore the trousers.

Dougie was first to break the silence.

"I'm afraid I'm away to bed about now, David. We trawler men have to get up early."

"That's fine," replied David. "I'm itching for a spot of bed myself."

They turned off the lights and walked upstairs, Dougie going to the bathroom and David to his little box room. A minute later, there was a tap on the door, and Dougie entered.

"I forgot tae ask," he began, a little nervously, David thought. "Did ye take off your wee pants under the kilt? We Scots don't allow them."

David said that he didn't, as all good Englishmen preferred to keep them on.

"Away with ye, ye don't know what you're missing," said Dougie. "Look at this."

He lifted his kilt up to reveal his manhood. David had never seen a large, white, freckled penis nestling in a shock of ginger pubic hair before, and he was in no particular rush to see another one.

"Oh, right," he gulped. "I see. I'll, erm, take them off later."

"Why not take them off now?" asked Dougie.

"I, erm, I've had an operation, you know, down there. I need them for support." David's hands felt clammy.

"The best thing for scars is fresh air," insisted Dougie. "Let me take them off for ye."

"I'm fine!" David assured him, edging around the wall.

"David, will ye toss ma wee caber then? It's the least ye can do after I've fed ye."

David was really sweating now. "I'm not keen on Highland games. Toss it yourself why don't you?"

Dougie looked hurt. "I thought you were, you know, that way, what with you travelling with Gordon."

"What?" asked David incredulously. "Gordon is a homosexual?"

"Well, bi-sexual actually."

"And the two young men on his boat?"

"Och, they're his sons, Hamish and Alan. He was married for years. Women are okay of course, but ye cannae beat the real thing!"

"Bloody hell!" said David, deeply uncomfortable. So you and Gordon were….."

"Aye! Many years back. Ye sound surprised, David. Did you no think Scotsmen could be that way too? Have ye no heard of the Gay Gordons?"

"Look!" said David desperately. "I'm really sorry to have misled you, if I did, and I'm grateful for dinner and everything, but I'm just not that way inclined, and if you're not, you're not. I hope you understand."

Dougie stood at the door, his sporran at a jaunty angle. "I'm sorry too," he sighed. "I'll no bother ye again tonight." He backed through the door and disappeared into his bedroom, his Highland fling thwarted.

David looked at himself in the broken old mirror above his sink and began to soliloquize.

"Dear God. Why can't it be someone else, just for a change? Why is it always me? I'm going to bed now, and I would appreciate it if you left me alone. At least till in the morning. Amen."

* * *

Dougie tapped on David's door at six-thirty. It was still dark. David sat bolt upright, terrified that it was about to begin again. Maybe Dougie's caber was ruling his head, and he was thinking about rape and pillage. The man was strong-looking. You had to be to work on a trawler boat.

"Yes?" he called nervously.

"I got ye a wee cup o' tea, David. It's time to be thinking about crossing to the mainland."

He came into the room with his head bowed and placed the tea on the bedside locker, avoiding eye contact as he did so.

"Can ye do me a big favour?" he asked sheepishly. "Forget all about last night please. My friends on the boat don't know."

David sipped his tea and nodded. Dougie walked silently back to the door.

"Oh Dougie," called David, just as his host disappeared behind the door. He popped his orange head into the room and smiled a sad smile.

“Yes?”

“If I’d got one that big, I’d show it off too!”

The two men chugged across the water, each wrapped up in their own thoughts. At the other end, Dougie helped David off the boat, pointed him in the direction of the train station and jumped back on board.

“Oh shit!” called David. “I’ve still got your kilt on. My jeans are in your box room!”

“It’s a souvenir from bonny Scotland, David,” he smiled. “Whenever you wear it, think o’ me, will ye?”

David shook his hand, and assured him that he would.

* * *

Feeling every bit the Highlander, David caught the train down to Fort William, where he was to change for Glasgow. He got out and decided to stretch his legs, as his connection wasn’t due for half an hour. As he stood blinking in the pleasant summer sunshine, he heard a familiar voice coming from the nearby café.

“Oi, Dave! Christ ode pal, yo’ve gone native!”

The Brummie and his mate walked over to meet him. At least, his mate did. The Brummie was hobbling with the aid of a stick.

“What happened to you?” asked David.

“I fell awkwardly on a rocky path up Ben Nevis and badly twisted my ankle. That’s why me and Nev are still here. We’re going home now though. The doc says I’m okay to travel.”

“Can I still hitch a lift?” asked David, affecting his best ‘lost puppy dog’ face.

“Course you can. It’ll save me havin’ to listen to this stupid bastard all the way home,” replied the Brummie.

“Took the words right out of me mouth!” laughed Nev.

Nev was lumbered with the driving, due to his friend's injury, so David sat beside him, leaving the Brummie to lie in the back and get some sleep. Everyone was feeling a little jaded from their various adventures in the Highlands, so the conversation during the first couple of hours was sparse, and usually along the lines of, 'look at that for a mountain!' After Glasgow, the Brummie began to sleep peacefully, and Nev decided to get some meaningful chat going.

"That's a nice kilt you've got on. I've always thought men looked good in kilts." He reached over and felt the material. "I bet that cost a few bob."

David coughed a nervous cough. This felt a little like déjà vu.

"Nev," he began. "Don't take offence, but you're not, erm, homosexual are you?"

The van screeched to a halt. Nev stared at the road. "Get out of the van, mate."

David quickly realized that his opening gambit could easily be misconstrued. "No, no, *I'm* not!"

"Pull the other one, pal. I should have realized when I saw a Black Country bloke in a skirt."

"No, listen! I've just had a bad experience at the hands of a Gay Gordon. I think he wanted me to suck a Fisherman's Friend. I just couldn't take that again."

Nev started up the van again and pulled away. "I'm surprised you took it the first time!"

"I didn't," said David, back-tracking furiously. "I legged it in the bloke's kilt. Funny though, I did feel very sorry for him, up there on his own."

Nev laughed a dirty laugh. "I bet it's great being stuck on a trawler with him and three thousand Mackerel in the middle of Dogger Bank."

"Yeah! He's got it hard."

"I reckon you got it hard for him! Did he ask you to blow on his bagpipe?"

"No, but he whipped his dirk out and threatened me with it!"

This was better; they were bonding now, Heteros against the Puffs. Wolves against the Albion; all of it total crap in David's eyes. Sometimes he appalled himself with his cowardly tactic of agreeing with whoever he was with at the time. He actually felt a lot of sympathy for Dougie, and liked the man well enough – he just drew the line at having to have sex with him. That said, if a bit of meaningless banter saved him from having to walk home from Glasgow he'd put up with it gladly. Principles were all fine and dandy, but they didn't get you back to Stourbridge.

"Just a minute," said Nev, as the three plastic primary-coloured cogs that made up his brain began to enmesh, "what were you doin' in his kilt in the first place?"

"Wow! Look at that for a mountain!" exclaimed David, desperate for a subject change. Nev gave him a suspicious look and drove on in silence.

Five tortuous hours later, the transit van was in Herefordshire, where the Brummie and Nev were staying overnight in order to visit Nev's parents. David was invited to hang around for a lift the following day, but he was understandably keen to get back so he could explain what had happened to him. He thanked his mountaineering friends for their help, and decided to try hitch-hiking, as he was low on cash after offering the Brummie petrol expenses, fully expecting him to politely refuse them. Unfortunately, he politely accepted, leaving David with one pound forty-six pence, a sizeable increase, at least, on what he set out with.

He stood on the roadside and breathed deeply to get some Herefordshire fresh air in his lungs, hoping that it would displace the toxic stuff he'd had to endure all the way from Fort William.

The Brummie and Nev were kind-hearted souls, but their digestive tracts needed serious medical attention. He cocked his thumb in the time-honoured way and began.

For the first half an hour, business was worryingly slow. One gentleman in a Jaguar had slowed down and offered a lift, but there was something about his fishnet tights and nail polish that had set off alarm bells in David's shrewd brain. After his exploits in the Mull of Kintyre, he had a nose for that kind of thing; a sort of sixth sense. Five minutes after Mr Fishnets had gone off in a huff, a rusty old Range Rover pulled into the lay-by. There were around five or six dark skinned, rough-looking characters in the vehicle, and they were towing a huge caravan.

"Where you off to then?" asked the driver.

"Stourbridge," replied David, somewhat nervously. He didn't fancy this bunch very much, and would have even chosen Mr Fishnets ahead of them, if push came to shove, and stark choices had to be made.

"Hop in," smiled the driver. He had gold teeth, an earring and greased back, curly black hair.

It was very difficult, having given them his desired destination, to then refuse their offer. It would have appeared churlish, and may have resulted in anger and bloodshed. He reluctantly stepped towards the Range Rover.

"Not in here. There ain't no fekkin' room, thicko. Get in the van."

David politely refused. "I didn't think that was legal, to travel in a caravan."

"Suit yourself," sneered the driver. "We're goin' down the M5 past Hagley, and that's very close to Stourbridge ain't it? Do you want a fekkin' lift or what? Ain't no skin off my nose."

Showing more of the iron resolve that he'd shown when Gordon offered him a whisky at breakfast time, he hopped in. The traveller closed the door after him and the convoy moved on. David was apprehensive. He'd taken an instant dislike to the men in the Range Rover and didn't trust them as far as he could throw them. He sat at the head of the caravan, looking at them as they drove along. The three in the back were swigging from cider bottles, and handing them over to the driver occasionally. Now and again, one would glance back at David, causing him to hastily look away to avoid eye contact. Jittery and restless, he began to rummage in the cupboards and drawers of the stark and empty caravan, looking for a magazine to occupy his time. The choice was poorer than a dentist's waiting room; just a dog-eared copy of Country Life and an obscure publication entitled Museums Monthly Magazine; (The magazine for Museum owners and Curators) cover story – A flexible shelving system to suit all room shapes. See page fourteen. Hardly the reading material to help the long winter evenings fly by. He chose Country Life. Inside was the usual section on houses for sale that no one other than Hugh Heffner could afford, followed by a society page, which consisted of photographs of Lady Isabella Toffee-Herbertson drinking champagne with her fiancé, Charles Double-Barrel-Bore and their la-di-da friends, after the recent stag shoot at Lord Chufnell Bufnell Tufnell's house in Surrey. David seethed quietly and turned the page. A photograph fell from the pages onto the floor. He stooped to pick it up, and was instantly struck by the likeness of the woolly, empty-headed and clown-like character in the picture, to his current employer, Percy Payne. A close inspection revealed a good reason for David's double-take. It *was* him.

This, by anyone's standards, was a coincidence. Why on earth would a traveller's caravan have a copy of Country Life on board for starters, let alone one with Percy's snapshot in it? He studied the photograph again. Percy was standing in front of a caravan, dressed in a Barbour coat. It was, unless David was very much mistaken (and he was quite often very much mistaken) the same caravan he was currently travelling in. Obviously, he'd sold it on after it got a little long in the tooth, and the gold-toothed gentleman had purchased it to go badger-baiting and cider-swigging in with his cronies.

The caravan seemed to be slowing down, so David put the magazines back in the drawer. He looked out of the window, and saw that the Range Rover had pulled into a service station, and was filling up with petrol. The caravan door opened, causing David to jump at least three feet off the seat and then affect a strange, overly relaxed pose by way of compensation.

Gold Teeth popped his head around the door. "Hey, Muggins. We're goin' to take a piss and get some grub for ten minutes. You stay here and guard the van, right? Don't get wandering off. Somebody might steal the fekker. It's easily done. I should know, 'cause I stole it in the first place!"

David laughed a nervous laugh.

"I'm not jokin' brother. We steal 'em, but woe betide anyone who steals from the Driscolls, know what I mean there nye?"

David gulped and assured him that he knew what he meant. Mr Driscoll sauntered off to join his brothers.

The oft referred-to gamut of emotions from A to Z began whizzing around David's head like stunt motorcyclists on the wall of death. David had seen this caravan before. He knew he had. He was certain that it was the old one that Percy's brother was about to renovate; the one he intended to use as a classroom. The photo of Percy and the Museum Magazine confirmed it. These travellers had stolen the Museum's caravan, and were brazenly pottering about the country in it and sticking two fingers up to the law, as usual. He opened the door, glanced around to see if anyone was watching, and tip-toed over to the Range Rover. Eureka! The keys were still in the ignition. These Driscolls were as cocky as they were lawless. He had three choices, and he needed to decide quickly. He could do a runner, phone the police, and wait for a lift from someone else. He could go back to the van and wait. This didn't appeal much. After all, the men were lawless. They'd probably only given him a lift in order to either rob him, rape him or use him for badger bait - maybe all three in the order named. His third choice was not only by far the most daring and heroic, but it also ensured that he got a lift straight to the museum.

He slipped into the driver's seat and started the engine, just as the Driscolls were leaving the café and walking towards him. They had obviously thought twice about staying for breakfast and elected to purchase a take-away. The walk turned into a run, as they realized that their vehicle was beginning to roll towards the exit. David rammed his foot down on the accelerator and screeched off the forecourt, the caravan lurching all over the tarmac behind him. He careered down the slip road, leaving the five travellers effing and blinding in a large cloud of blue air, caused in equal part by the emissions from the Range Rover's engine and the Driscoll's foul language.

Still sweating and shaking as a result of his actions, David kangarooed along the M5, crossing lanes left right and centre. He had never driven anything larger than a Mini Clubman in his life, and he wasn't exactly brilliant with one of those. It was, therefore, a marginally less worried David Day that left the M5 motorway at the slip road for Hagley. All he had left to negotiate now was a few miles of quiet country road, Stourbridge town centre and the suburbs that surrounded it, and finally the half-mile stretch that led to Stanmore Castle. He would arrive to a hero's welcome, and no doubt Percy would throw his arms around him and cry, 'My beamish boy!' He was almost home and dry now, and nothing could go wrong if he kept his head, and concentrated on the width of the vehicle.

As he swerved erratically around Stourbridge Ring Road, he became cognizant of a worrying noise. It sounded like the siren of an ambulance, no doubt on its way to some poor old chap who'd suffered a heart attack. David tried to look in his rear-view mirrors, but the huge caravan behind him was obscuring his vision. He continued on his way, realizing that the ring road had three lanes, which meant the ambulance wasn't being held up by him, at least. The siren was very close now, and sounded almost as if it were inside the caravan. A second later, a police panda car was alongside him, with a rather flushed-looking bobby inside, telling him to pull over. This, with a heavy heart, he duly did.

The two policemen walked over to the Range Rover and asked him to wind down his window. David smiled sweetly at the officers, as his father had instructed him. The smile changed to open-mouthed shock when he recognized the owners of the peaked caps.

"Well well well!" began Donald. (This, for the sake of clarity, was not the fictional Highland character, Donald, who lost his troosers, but a flesh and blood Stourbridge police officer of the same name.)

"Thrice hello!" said Pongo, a man who obviously didn't like to waste time with meaningless small talk. "David Day. We have you at last. Can you step out of the vehicle please?"

Donald, meanwhile, had begun to chat excitedly to base on his walkie-talkie. American sheriffs went though very much the same emotions when they finally apprehended Billy the Kid.

David got out and stood on the pavement.

"Well I never," he sighed, "the Keystone Cops. Long time no see. What have I done this time?"

Donald's face was sadder and more serious than usual. This surprised David a little. Normally there was a little good-natured banter on these occasions.

"David, I don't know what you were thinking of this time. We are going to have to arrest you for stealing this caravan from Stanmore Castle. There have also been serious accusations made about you in regard to an attack on a librarian in Kinver on Tuesday, and another assault on a man in the High Street who tried to apprehend you. I'm sorry son, but this time it's no laughing matter. You are under arrest."

For once, David was utterly speechless. He could, of course, defend himself against all of the charges, but they were so complicated to explain, and he just didn't know where to begin. Pongo looked at David with that 'I'm disappointed with you - you, of all people' kind of look, and slipped on the cuffs. David asked if that was absolutely necessary, and Pongo assured him that it was.

"Fair enough," replied David, shell-shocked to the core. "That's the last time you come round my place and eat all my Hobnobs then."

David was an amateur psychologist, and he knew full well how to hurt Pongo. It was the officer's turn to look shell-shocked now.

"Look, we're sorry, Dave," interjected Donald. We know you're not a bad lad, but we have to do our job. We've had an 'all-stations missing person alert' out for you, nationwide. The librarian has accused you of just about everything, including attempted murder. You disappeared off the face of the earth and now we see you riding around in a stolen caravan. Come on Dave! It's going to have to be a good story this time, even by your bloody standards!"

* * *

It was Friday morning at nine o'clock a.m., when the Range Rover and caravan, driven by Donald and Pongo, pulled onto the gravel in front of Stanmore Castle. Julian, Percy, Glenda and Jethro came running out to greet it.

"Officers!" beamed Percy. "You found it! Thank you *so* much."

The rear door of the vehicle swung open and David emerged still wearing his kilt.

“Morning folks! Have ye no missed me?” he asked, affecting an outrageously inaccurate Scottish accent.

“Where the f…” began Julian, utterly bewildered

“The Highlands of Scotland, for those of ye who are interested,” came his timely interruption. “It’s a long story, Julian, so put the wee kettle on.”

And with that, he sauntered into the castle with a dopey grin fixed to his stupid face.

* * *

“I have to hand it to them,” said David, sipping his tea in Julian’s little office, glad to be where he belonged once more, “for all Donald and Pongo’s faults, and believe me, there are many, this time they sorted everything out with commendable speed. My story must have been complex for them to comprehend, to say the least, especially with their negligible intellects, but to be fair, they got the gist - at least, Donald did – Pongo slept through most of it. The incident at the library was a bit unfortunate, but when they looked into what her reading matter was, they came to the conclusion that she was a bit of a fantasist with an over-active imagination.”

“Nothing like you then?”

“They also persuaded the mad bloke to drop all charges by threatening counter charges against *him*. He’s been exposing himself on a regular basis and there are lots of witnesses.”

“And *you’ve* only exposed yourself once, which is neither here nor there.”

“Anyway, enough about me. What’s been going on around here in my absence?”

Julian's demeanour changed noticeably as he realized that he was expected to recount his recent ghastly experiences. In one way, David's re-appearance had helped greatly. He had not, after all, crumbled to dust and vanished because of using Rametup's comb as suspected, which did wonders for Julian's frayed nerves, but there was no escaping the awful apparition that he'd witnessed the other night. Where was the explanation for that, and for the real severed finger? He gave David the gory details, omitting no detail, however slight. It was a shocked and deeply troubled David Day that sat before him now, hanging on his every word.

"That's marvellous!" he began, once the power of speech had returned to him. "I may not have actually crumbled to dust yet, but what if it's imminent? I could be painting the mural this afternoon, and you come along with a cup of tea for me, and there I am, a little pile on the floor."

"Don't be silly," replied Julian. "When have I ever brought you a cup of tea? Look, we need to travel together, watch each other's backs; be vigilant. I'm sure there must be some logical explanation for what I saw, but I'm damned if I know what it is. I'm sure it stems from the ashabtis that Percy found in the loft. All this started when he discovered them. They're pure evil, I tell you, and I'm not generally superstitious. I swear, when I came in here not long ago, there was an unearthly stench coming off them. I vote we sling 'em in the canal and stick with Elton and the gang."

"I can put your mind at rest about the stench anyway," said David. "That was Pongo. He came in here to use the phone, and I recognize the aroma. It's still lingering, even now. Anyway, there's no such thing as mummies, so get that out of your head will you? It was probably just a bad dream, which is understandable."

"No such thing as mummies? The Valley of the Kings is full of them, you cretin! How can you say that?"

"I mean living, Boris Karloff-type mummies, you loony. Now calm down, attend to your school trip, and I'll carry on with my mural."

Julian had forgotten about the school trip. Brierley Bank Juniors had booked a return visit, and he was dreading it. He would rather have entertained St Trinians on one of their more playful days than have had Brierley Bank back again, after the last time. He rushed off to erect the barricades, and left David to get on with it. David was just pleased to be back. He'd set off on Tuesday to visit the library, and ended up touring the Highlands of Scotland. He was like Dorothy from the Wizard of Oz and Alice in Wonderland all rolled into one. At least now he could settle down and catch up a bit, as long as Julian kept the little brats away.

It was eight-thirty that evening before David laid down his brushes. Like Julian, he didn't have a lady friend to go home to, at least not until Sunday, so he was content to work late and make up for lost time. Julian arrived looking more harassed than usual, carrying two cold bottles of beer.

"That's enough for today, Leonardo," he smiled wearily. "Come and join me in my den for a drop of anaesthetic. If I'm ever tempted to have kids, do me a favour and whack my bollocks with two building bricks."

"Hard day?" David asked, tumbling into the office and slumping exhausted into the comfy chair.

"Very. Those bastards are always up to something. You can't take your eyes off 'em. What about you?"

"Good. I've nearly finished the blacksmith's shop now. Here comes Percy."

The door creaked open, and in came not Percy, but Hitlerina, bearing gifts.

Julian's face drained of colour. "You look, I don't want to."

David picked it up and examined it. “It’s a shrivelled old sausage by the looks of it. Shit, no! Sausages don’t have nails. It’s another bloody human finger!”

He dropped it on the floor as if it were red-hot, and a colourless Julian tidily put it with the other one in his drawer, wearing one of his Marigold kitchen gloves. He then sheepishly asked David if he fancied staying the night with him, just for a bit of company. David politely refused, stating that he’d had a similar experience in Scotland and it had not turned out happily. After several firm rebuttals of David’s implied allegation, plus a little unmanly begging, Julian finally persuaded David to agree. It would, he tried to kid himself, be fun, like spending a night in a haunted house. Julian blanched at the expression and swigged on his beer bottle in an animated way.

Dinner, by Julian’s standards, was a lavish affair. He’d popped to the local convenience store that stayed open till eleven, and procured two chicken and mushroom pies and bags of frozen oven chips and peas. David supplied the wine, choosing a Pinot Grigio, a pleasant reminder of Italy, a place he had grown to love whilst forging renaissance drawings at Lord Hickman’s apartment. He could put up with the rancid chicken pies and oven chips, but he was damned if he was going to drink Julian’s German muck. The curtains were drawn - just to create atmosphere, insisted David’s host - and candles were lit.

“Are you sure you’re not trying to get off with me?” asked David sarcastically. “You’ll be measuring me for a kilt next.”

Julian wasn’t listening, however. He was staring at the curtains again.

“Shush!” he whispered. “Did you hear that?”

David said that he didn’t and carried on eating. Julian paused once more and cocked an ear. There was definitely something prowling around just outside the window. He grabbed his old cricket bat from the cloak room and handed David a badminton racquet, for which David thanked him brokenly, adding a little sarcastically that it would be useful for when he, the mummy and a couple of passing werewolves fancied a game of mixed doubles.

Julian approached the curtains with his finger to his lips, and then dramatically yanked them aside. Hitlerina stood gazing at them with something in her mouth, demanding to be let in. Julian quickly opened the French windows and allowed the cat and around half a dozen fat moths to enter, which didn't please David one iota, as he was, to use his suspect terminology, 'moth-ophobic'. The cat shimmied around Julian's legs, as was her custom before scaring him half to death, and laid down her latest offering for him to scrutinize. The curator confirmed that it was not a finger, whereupon his companion breathed a sigh of relief. Whoever was doling out the fingers must have been running low, and decided to put a stop to it. This time, the anonymous body-parts donor had sent a human toe.

"That's it!" wailed Julian, beside himself. "First thing tomorrow, I'm calling the police. This has gone beyond a joke now."

David examined the grisly shrivelled flesh, and shuddering with sheer revulsion, flicked it into some kitchen roll to show the boys in blue.

"I've got an idea. Why don't we follow Hitlerina tomorrow, and see if we can work out where she's getting this stuff from. Perhaps there's a churchyard around here."

"Oh don't!" moaned Julian. "Now I'll have nightmares. Besides, I know where she's getting them from. She's following the mummy around that came to my window last night, and grabbing the bits that fall off him."

He got hold of the cat by the scruff of her neck and escorted her to the back door. "She can bugger off out with her mummy friend, and I'm not letting her lick the back of my hand anymore."

He opened the door, kicked her out and closed it again, all within the space of a split second. The two friends tried to resume their supper, but the food was cold and uninviting now, as distinct from the hot and uninviting state it had been in before Hitlerina arrived. They decided on an early night, followed by a hearty breakfast at the village's Maori Coffee Shop to make up for the calories lost.

As both of them walked upstairs in close formation, it was inevitable that thoughts of the Hitchcock film, Psycho, sprang to mind. They cleaned their teeth together, peed together and, after a full and frank discussion, slept together.

David slept but fitfully, tossing and turning, and pulling Julian's sheets off. He dreamt about a large black catfish, writhing and squealing on a lawn, with its fins hacked off and seeping blood. As a consequence of this, he suddenly awoke, shouting incoherent rubbish and sweating profusely, scaring Julian rigid in the process. Needing the lavatory, as usual, and unable to put it off any longer, he tip-toed out of the bedroom across the landing, looking left and right as he did so, before dashing to pull the light cord in the bathroom. After relieving himself, he paused on the landing, convinced that he'd heard a dull thudding noise downstairs.

Glancing nervously down the staircase, he saw, to his absolute horror, an Egyptian mummy staring back at him, climbing one step at a time, slowly and methodically, his bandaged hands grasping the rails. Petrified to the brink of heart failure, David somehow managed to turn and flee into the bedroom, unable even to scream. He shook Julian violently, scaring him half to death for the second time in five minutes, and found his voice.

"The mummy. It's coming to get us, up the stairs, NOW!"

Julian grabbed his cricket bat from beside the bed and dashed out onto the landing, displaying great, if unexpected, courage. His razor-sharp mind had decided that, if they were to stand any chance against the powers of darkness, it was best to knock seven shades of shit out of them with a cricket bat while they were still climbing the stairs and vulnerable.

Psyched up now and fearing no one, he let fly with a blood-curdling Ninja scream, holding his bat like a samurai sword.

Alas, it was all in vain. The mummy was not there.

“You twat!” whined Julian, somewhat insensitively. “You were just having a bad dream.”

“Au contraire,” insisted David, shaking visibly. “I know a dream when I see one. My dream was about catfish with severed fins, if you don’t mind. I was wide awake when I went to the loo, and I’ve never sleep-walked in my life. There was a bloody mummy climbing the stairs, pal - It was bandaged, with horrible, staring eyes and it was flipping evil.”

## CHAPTER 8

## A Plague on Both your Houses

Lord Hickman sat in the waiting room, reading 'Homes & Gardens'. A pretty nurse coughed politely and informed him that Doctor Hess would see him now. He dropped the magazine back onto the glass coffee table and walked into the doctor's lavish Harley Street office.

"Ah, Lord Hickman!" the doctor exclaimed. "Sit down will you. Let me look at you." He approached him from the back, and from his top pocket pulled a sharp pair of scissors, which he used to snip a section of band-aid. "I trust you have been taking it easy as I instructed. The painkillers I gave you are very effective, but they can sometimes affect the balance of one's mind."

He peeled away at the bandage as if he were removing the skin from an orange, slowly and carefully, revealing more and more face as he did so.

"Excellent, excellent! The scars are healing beautifully. It's down to your fine, aristocratic face, I'm sure. There now, that's all. Now let me see your hands." He repeated the procedure. "Again, excellent. Now, my friend, you can put your robbing fingers wherever you like. You have no fingerprints!"

Lord Hickman stood and admired his new look in the mirror. "The bruising is subsiding nicely, I must say, but you know, this is so weird. I'm looking into your mirror, and a complete stranger is looking back at me. He's still devilishly handsome of course, but with this new nose, my moustache gone, and my dyed blond hair, I could be a German prince, or maybe a member of the Swedish aristocracy! I am very impressed, Doctor Hess, very impressed. Even my mother wouldn't know me, but then again, she hasn't wanted to know me for a good many years."

Doctor Hess smiled a sour smile. "I am pleased that you are pleased. I now consider that we are square, and don't take offence, but I'd rather I never saw you again."

"No offence taken. Consider our little arrangement concluded, and in future, try to pick girlfriends that are over fourteen."

Lord Hickman bade him farewell and swept out of the doctor's consulting rooms with a smarmy, self-satisfied look on his brand-new face.

Doctor Hess sat down at his desk and fumed. "You may have a new head, but you will always be a short-arsed little shit," he growled, and buzzed for his next patient.

* * *

The eleven-thirty-five Euston train to Birmingham New Street left the station, just for a change, bang on time. The journey usually took around an hour and thirty-five minutes, which gave Lord Hickman ample time to mull over his battle plan. Having already been in the Midlands, it was an inconvenience to have to return to London just so that the bloated cradle-snatching Kraut could remove his bandages and check him over. That said, it had to be done, and the results were worth the effort.

Being stuck in prison for five years was a damned inconvenience too, but it did give one the opportunity to pick up a few new contacts, not to mention practical skills. If one didn't know how to break into a stately home before one went inside, one most certainly did by the time one was released. Lord Hickman's little black book now contained an impressive list of useful artisans and craftsmen. He was on first name terms with burglars, con-artists, bent solicitors and accountants, art forgers and ex-coppers, and he'd got something on most of them, which saved him from ever paying the going rate.

All this was fine and dandy of course, but what he really needed was cash. There was precious little left to keep him in the style to which he had previously been accustomed, and this couldn't be allowed to continue. Luckily, he had a plan, but so far, there had been serious problems with its execution. Since his operation, he had been staying in rented accommodation near the village of Tutton on Stour, namely a very small and sparsely-furnished cottage on a farmer's estate. It was hardly the standard of housing a Lord should have to endure, but it was cheap, and extremely private. He had informed his landlord that he was a reclusive novelist who hated interruptions or company of any kind, and was prone to come and go without warning, depending on his whims. The farmer had assured him on the phone that he didn't care one iota if he never clapped eyes on him, so long as the cheque didn't bounce, and he didn't trash the cottage. Lord Hickman paid for his stay in advance, and had so far been the model tenant, which pleased the landlord no end, as, being a farmer, he had also been brought up to be anti-social and money-grabbing. It was a shame, in a way, that the two men were never to meet. They were kindred spirits.

The heavily-bandaged aristocrat had arrived at the cottage under the cover of darkness, and stayed in during daylight hours to avoid frightening the natives. His supplies were delivered to the place by the local supermarket, and a cheque was always pinned to the front door for the driver. Now, at last, he could venture out once more, to wander around town or eat out at a restaurant, secure in the knowledge that no one would recognize him. To complete his radical transformation, he had also been practising a new skill in his prison cell, and now it was nigh-on perfect. Lord

Hickman no longer had an upper-crust accent. For the time being, at least, he was a Brummie.

Barn Owl Cottage, though Spartan, had one great advantage. It was a ten minute walk through the farmer's field and across Tutton Common to an infinitely grander property – Stanmore Castle. Impatient to re-possess a sentimental item that he had been forced to leave behind, due to his unforeseen arrest and subsequent imprisonment, Lord Hickman had foolishly trodden this route twice that week, before he was fit and ready. The plastic surgeon, he had to begrudgingly admit, had been right. The painkillers had made him a little addled, and he had gone off half-cocked, almost jeopardizing the entire operation. Still heavily bandaged, and wearing his old black overcoat to keep warm, he had succeeded in getting as far as the old stable block when a man he didn't recognize scared the living daylights out of him by suddenly pulling open the curtains and screaming like a deranged fishwife. The following evening he had tried again, and this time got into the building, thinking that no one was at home, only to have another crazed lunatic frighten him half to death at the top of the stairs. This last incident had been far worse than the previous night, as Lord Hickman had recently watched Alfred Hitchcock's Psycho on television, and the memory was vivid.

As he ran back to his humble rented cottage across the muddy, moonlit field, his heart still pounding from the shock of it, the image of the long-haired demon at the top of the stairs came back to haunt him. He knew that face – he was sure of it. At first, he couldn't bring to mind where he'd seen it before, and then, as he dashed into the sanctity of his cottage and locked the door behind him, he finally realized whom it belonged to. It was that bastard, David Day – the one who was responsible for robbing him of his precious freedom. He was obviously living at Stanmore Castle now, after the rightful owner had been cruelly incarcerated.

Now Lord Hickman suddenly had two reasons to get into the castle. He had to retrieve something that he'd hidden there, and there was also an old score to settle with his arch enemy. After much thought, he decided to abandon his original plan, which was to break into the stable block after dark. It was far too risky, now that the place appeared to be co-inhabited by two highly-strung homosexuals. Besides, trying to find an old key in the dark was almost impossible. He had to find a way of getting into the place under false pretences, and be left to rummage, but this was a tall order. Alternatively, he needed to plant someone in the castle, to rummage for him; someone that the current owner trusted. There was a germ of an idea forming, but there were many risks involved. He purchased an undrinkable coffee from the passing refreshments trolley and mulled the situation over all the way to Birmingham.

* * *

"Have you ever been fishing, Jools?" asked David, apropos of nothing, as the curator stood watching him paint.

"No," replied Julian. "If I'm ever tempted, I just get out a tin of white emulsion and paint a museum wall. The effect that watching it dry has on me is broadly the same."

"You miss the point," sighed David, shaking his head sadly. "It's not just about man versus fish. It's also about meditation and stress relief, and you and I need some of that, I can tell you. The principle of fishing is thus; you spend hours just staring, trance-like at your little pink tip. Then suddenly it starts jerking furiously, and you get very excited indeed."

"Sounds like my love life."

"How droll. It's great, trust me. I used to go with my dad on the Teme, in Tenbury Wells, and I suppose that's why it brings back fond memories. I notice that Percy has got all the gear. Why don't we go down to the castle lake after work for a couple of hours, to take our minds off the mummy and the body parts? I might be lucky and catch you a trout. It's better than frozen cod every night."

Julian took the bait, and was now hooked. "Okay then, Isaac Walton. Tonight after work, but you'll have to show me what to do."

"Fantastic!" grinned David. "It's my last night of freedom before Suzanne gets back, so I thought I'd spend some time with you. It's the least I can do, now we're sleeping together. I'll ask Jethro to run into town and buy us some bait."

"Talking of whom," added Julian, "I'm a bit worried about him and Glenda."

"Why's that?"

"Well, have you seen them lately? Glenda is getting more and more butch by the day, and Jethro is growing his hair long."

David was offended. "I've got long hair. It's fashionable, in case you hadn't noticed."

"I know that, dimwit. It's just that Jethro's hair looks a bit girly, that's all. Talking of hair, what's that in yours?"

David flicked at his hair nervously. He could tell by Julian's tone that whatever it was, it was alive. A large, sandy-coloured locust hopped from his coiffure onto the museum floor.

"Bloody hell!" shrieked David. "Ever since I was at school, I've hated those things! I didn't think you could get them in England."

"Neither did I," agreed Julian, "But there's another one!" A locust was eyeing them up from the sleeve of Elton's smock. A further inspection revealed two more in Elton's wig, six on the radiator and three inside the blacksmith's apron. Julian, who was slightly less squeamish about insects than David, gathered them up in a large Victorian sweet jar. After an hour's search, there were sixty-seven, and undoubtedly more to come.

This infestation, had it occurred even the week before, would have been regarded by Julian as no more than a nuisance, but now it had a deeper and darker significance that filled him with a nameless fear. Brother Adrian had spelt out the various forms that Rametup's curse would take, and he had been deadly accurate. He had prophesied disappearances and been right; David may have escaped crumbling to dust, but Lord Henry Hickman, his wife and butler had all copped it, and were never seen again. There was talk of plague, and lo and behold, the locusts had arrived, the traditional 'plague du jour' in Egypt. Julian couldn't wait for the fires to start. Then they'd have the full set.

The famously un-superstitious curator returned to his office, unaware that the locusts had come, not from Egypt, but from four miles down the road at Brierley Bank School, where they had previously lived in the biology lab's glass tanks, before Joey Atkins (6R) discovered a new use for Tupperware lunch boxes.

Once the locusts had been released into the wild - if Tutton Common could be described as 'wild' - Julian phoned the local police and requested an officer to come and take away the various fingers and toes he'd been amassing, for analysis. He had rather fancied allowing Hitlerina to gradually collect the full set, but Percy had insisted that he didn't want them hanging around the place, attracting flies. No sooner had he replaced the receiver, when the telephone rang. It was a gentleman with a strong Birmingham accent, asking if he could have a word with Jethro.

This was odd. In all Julian's time as curator, no one had ever wanted a word with Jethro. He told the caller to hold, and ran down the hall and out of the front door. Jethro was carrying a wheel barrow full of horse shit from point A to point B. The gormless gardener set it down and ran into the castle, leaving his disgusting footprints all over the polished tiled floor. He arrived breathless at the office, and Julian, who prided himself on his manners, vacated the room and closed the door to allow him some privacy.

"That you Jethro?" asked the caller. Jethro said that it was. The affected Birmingham accent was immediately replaced by a very upper-crust one. "Jethro, remember me? I want you to be quiet and just listen for the time being. This is Lord Hickman, your old employer. You'll be pleased, no doubt, to hear that I am once more a free man, give or take the odd visit to my parole officer. However, enough about me. How are you?"

Jethro was stunned, though the casual observer would not have noticed much difference. "Er, all-roit, thank you sir!"

"Good! How's the cross-dressing coming along?"

Jethro reddened and looked awkward. He had no verbal response. Five years previously, Lord Hickman had been out for a day at the races, and had arrived home earlier than expected, to find his gardener in his wife's bedroom trying on her clothing, and in full make-up. The incident had been deeply embarrassing, and Jethro was given a written warning. It had never been mentioned since, until now.

"Come come, Jethro," he continued. "Cat got your tongue? Now listen, I need you to do me a big favour, and this must go no further. There is a largish and very ornate key somewhere in the castle, and I need it. It's around eight inches in length, and it has a very distinctive 'H' design which forms the business end. It used to be in the old stable block, where the vineyard offices were, in the old writing desk. Do you know where I mean?"

Jethro nodded. Not a fat lot of use during a phone conversation.

"I need you to get it and drop it into the old milk churn near the back gates. If it is no longer where I told you, I will need you to rummage through the drawers elsewhere until it is found. This is very important. Do this for me, and I will say nothing to anyone about your strange habits. Do you understand me?"

Jethro swallowed hard, and croaked his response. The line went dead. He replaced the receiver, and the phone instantly rang again. This time it was Suzanne, asking to speak to David. Jethro, still reeling, staggered out of the office and informed Julian, who was waiting patiently outside, that David's fiancée was calling him. David, who had been busy painting his mural, ran down the corridor and picked up the phone.

"Hi!" said Suzanne cheerfully.

"Hello," replied David. "How's things in Solihull?"

"I'm not in Solihull," laughed Suzanne. "Get this, I'm in Spain."

David could make nothing of this. "Did I hear you correctly? Did you say Spain?"

"Yes. I hope you don't mind. As you know, I went home because it was my folks' silver wedding anniversary. Well dad, bless him, surprised mum with a week's holiday in Spain to celebrate, and he's invited me as well, free of charge. It was all a big surprise. We didn't know till an hour before we set off for the airport! I said you'd be okay without me for another week, as you were probably busy at the museum, and it is a once in a lifetime thing, after all!"

David said that he didn't mind at all. If he was truthful, he was enjoying the novelty of being on his own.

"It's weird," continued Suzanne. "One minute I was in England, ready to get back home, and the next I'm in Spain. Don't you think it's unbelievable how you can wake up in another country, just like that?"

"Yes," agreed David, who had had some experience of this himself.

"Anyway, must keep it brief. Dad's paying the phone bill. How's the hernia?"

"Much better, thanks. I only scream once a day now."

"Anything happened of interest up your end, so to speak?"

“No. Not really.”

“Okay, must go, kiss kiss!” The phone went dead. Just as David replaced the receiver, the phone rang again. It was the police station, informing them that a couple of officers would arrive shortly to collect the body parts.

Julian popped his head around the door to ask if there was any chance of having his room back in the foreseeable future. The place was getting more like a small outpost of Interpol than a curator’s office.

* * *

Jethro arrived back from the tackle shop just after six o’clock with a pint of writhing multi-coloured maggots in, of all things, a Tupperware lunchbox, obviously the container of choice for the fashion-conscious insect. David downed tools, declaring that he’d had more than enough for one day, prompting Julian to make some caustic comment about Michelangelo putting in far longer days, and on his back, to boot. David responded with a line about Michelangelo being paid a damned sight more than he was, which, in turn, prompted Percy, who was passing through en-route to the Fox Inn to call ‘Fifteen Love’. David asked him if they could borrow his fishing equipment, and with a regal wave, he told them to help themselves. Jethro, who was only paid till six, decided to join them, as he too was partial to a spot of fishing.

Ten minutes later, they were assembled at the old ‘Monet Bridge’, a beautiful construction which Lord Hickman had installed on the edge of the lake, inspired by famous Monet lily pond paintings, which he greatly admired. David assembled two rods, threaded on the floats and tied the hooks. He tried the floats in the lake, and adjusted the lead shot until each float sat nice and low in the water. Jethro, who was a regular angler, knew how to prepare his own equipment.

“Now we are ready to begin,” smiled David, eager to show off his skills to the novice Julian. “Pass me a maggot or two.”

“Sod off!” replied Julian, cringing. “I’m not touching them.”

“They’re not as bad as bloody locusts!” David assured him. “What’s up with you, you big girl?”

For a fleeting moment, Jethro appeared wounded, but carried on preparing his line. David tut-tutted loudly and picked them up himself. He attached them to the hook and cast it into the lake, showing Julian how to release the bale arm so that the line would slide off the spool. Then he threw a few maggots into the water around the float, to attract attention. Remarkably, within a few seconds, the float disappeared beneath the water, and David struck. He could tell by the electric vibrations in his rod that he’d hooked something, and a decent-sized one at that. Jethro, amazed at David’s speedy result, abandoned his own rod and grabbed the landing net. First blood to David, a nice perch, unhooked without a fuss and delivered to the safety of the keep net.

Julian was now eager to participate. He was beginning to see something in this fishing lark after all. David baited his hook for him, as he sheepishly owned up to being squeamish about impaling the maggots. He was about to try his first cast, when David told him to be quiet, and look into the water under the bridge.

“Look! Just there,” he whispered, “a massive carp. Bloody hell! It’s *huge*. If you can drop your line in just there, you might hook a monster.”

Julian reached over the bridge to get a better view and looked down. His spectacles went plop, into the water, and the shy carp scarpered.

“Oh shit!” he moaned. “My new glasses! I’ve only had them two days.”

David gave him one of his looks. The man hadn’t even had one cast, and already there was a major problem.

“I have to get them back, David,” he insisted. “They cost me a fortune.”

“Well don’t ask me to retrieve them,” replied David. “I can’t swim. Are they metal? If they are, we could try a magnet, if we had one.”

“We *do* have one!” said Julian. “The science exhibit has got one of those great big red horseshoe ones. Do us a favour, Jethro. Pop up and grab it will you? There’s a dear!”

Jethro ran back to the museum and returned, breathless, five minutes later, wielding a magnet that looked capable of lifting the bridge out of the lake, let alone a pair of spectacles. As he handed it over, David noticed how nice his eyes looked that evening. If there wasn’t a hint of mascara there, he was a Dutchman. He tied the magnet to his line and dropped it carefully into the water where the specs had fallen.

“This may seem a long shot,” he said, but I’ve known people do this before, with some success. I just hope your glasses aren’t some weird alloy that magnets won’t stick to.”

David’s first attempt was an abject failure. Undaunted, he tried once more. Again, nothing.

“Let me try,” suggested Julian. “I think I know where they fell. He lowered the magnet into the water carefully, to avoid smashing the spectacles, and wiggled the rod back and forth.

“Eureka!” he cried. “I’ve definitely got a bite. Unless it’s a metallic Trout, these are my specs.” He lifted the rod slowly, and pulled out not a pair of spectacles but a rusty key, with an ‘H’ shaped end.

“Well I never!” he smiled. “Another exhibit for Percy. Lord knows where this came from.” He removed the key and tried again. Half an hour later, his patience was rewarded, and the errant specs were retrieved, none the worse for their underwater adventure.

“I’d better get off home,” said Jethro. “Shall oi put the key somewhere for you, Julian?”

“Oh, thanks Jeth. Drop it on my office desk on the way out will you? Dave and I are going to have a fishing contest. I’m damned if I’m going to let him beat me.”

Jethro walked into the office and closed the door behind him, his feeble mind in turmoil. What he had just witnessed was nothing short of a miracle. He had been set a mission to find a needle in a haystack, and the good Lord had rewarded him by issuing forth the very key from the depths of Davy Jones’s locker, bang on cue!

Jethro hated Lord Hickman for what he’d said, and much preferred his new employer, but he saw no alternative to purloining the key. The only potential problem was that Julian would surely enquire as to its whereabouts the following day, and the finger would point at the gardener. Glancing around the untidy office, he noticed a large lump of Plasticine, which Julian liked to play with while he was on the phone. Jethro had seen spies in films use modelling clay to make impressions from keys, and surely, he reasoned, this was similar. Dividing the lump into two parts, he rolled them out into sausage shapes and flattened them out on the table. He then made impressions of both sides of the key, and carefully wrapped his handiwork in kitchen roll, before furtively tip-toeing out of the castle, en-route for the milk churn. He dropped the parcel inside, with a hastily scribbled note.

*‘Deer Lord Hickman, this was the best I cood do,*

*as key will be mist and thay’ll no hoo nicked it.*

*Now can you leave me alone please? Jethro.’*

Down at the lake, David and Julian were having a productive time. No one had fished the waters since Lord Hickman’s day, and it was teeming with all manner of creatures that weren’t fussy about being caught as long as there was a maggot in it for them. The tally, by half-past eight, was ten to David and six to Julian; not bad for a rank amateur. They agreed that fading light should stop play, packed away the rods and began to plan dinner, now that David's girlfriend was no longer coming home that evening. They decided against another night in at Julian's place, blaming the inedible food and the recent spate of mummy sightings, and instead voted for a night at the Fox Inn. After a reasonable meal and far too much Tutton Ale, they decided to stay at David and Suzanne's new house, which not only boasted two bedrooms, but a singular lack of zombified ancient Egyptians.

Lord Hickman, by contrast, had not had such a good evening. Assuming his Birmingham accent once more, he was on the phone, awaiting Jethro, who had been carrying some horse shit from point B to point C when the call came. He shut himself in Julian's office, fully expecting hearty congratulations from his ex-employer for a job well done. It was something of a shock, therefore, when none came.

"Jethro, can you speak?"

"Yes sir, there's nobody about."

"Good, you bloody cretin. I emptied out the churn and a melted blob of shit landed on the courtyard, a poor substitute for the key I was looking forward to receiving. Did you *drop* it into the churn, by any chance?

"Yes sir, because you told me to."

"I told you to drop the key, moron, not a lump of clay. After a lump of clay falls three feet, it seldom looks pristine. Add to that the hottest day of the year so far, coupled with my tipping the churn upside down and shaking it, and you have a completely worthless lump of shit; in fact, a little like you."

"Sorry sir, but…."

"I know. You told me. They'd know the key was missing. I am now going to change to plan B, so listen carefully. Today, in a while, I am going to create a diversion. Whilst everyone is being diverted, you will take the key and drop it in the milk churn. Do you understand me?"

Jethro said that he did, and enquired as to the precise nature of the diversion, so that he would know when to act. Lord Hickman assured him that even someone as dim-witted as Jethro would know when it was happening, and curtly put the phone down. It was less than half an hour later when the plumes of thick black smoke began to rise from the old stables. The workmen who were converting part of the stables into a tearoom were first to notice it, and they raised the alarm. Within seconds, Percy, Julian, David and Glenda were in the courtyard, horror-struck. Julian, in particular was visibly emotional, as it was his flat that was on fire. Within minutes the smoke had thickened and was belching out of the disintegrating roof tiles, accompanied by frightening tongues of orange flame. The fire brigade had already been summoned by a quick-thinking builder, but Percy had another thing on his mind. He warned everyone to stay outside, and raced back into the main castle building to rescue Bertie and Hitlerina, just in case the conflagration spread. Jethro was also currently unaccounted for, but, he hoped and prayed that his gardener was somewhere in the extensive grounds, shovelling his manure.

Percy called his beloved dog by name, but there was no response. Frantic now, he charged down the corridor to Julian's office, a favourite resting place for both animals, and his intuition had not been wrong. Sleeping under the desk, Bertie and his feline friend were oblivious to the drama unfolding in the courtyard. As Percy burst in on his gallant mission, he was surprised to see find that another dumb animal was in need of rescuing. Jethro was rifling through the drawers, and he had guilt written all across his freshly-depilated face. A more suave customer than he could easily have bluffed his way out of the situation, but Jethro was out of his depth, and he knew that Percy knew that he was up to no good. His face crumpled, and leaked the first of many tears.

"Oi'm sorry Mr Percy. Oi've let you down. You've been so good to me, keepin' me on and all, and oi've let you down."

"We can discuss this later, Jethro," replied Percy, disappointed. "Right now, let's get outside in case the wind carries the fire into the castle."

Percy and his three dumb chums made for the exit. It was a tear-stained and forlorn Jethro that sat slumped against the castle wall watching the fire engines tackle the blaze. Luckily, if it could be called lucky, the fire had been contained, and though it spelt disaster for the stable block, Julian's flat, his worldly possessions and the embryonic tea rooms, at least the grand old castle had survived.

Percy thanked the firemen brokenly, and they informed him that a fire investigator would be calling as soon as possible, to ascertain if the fire had been an accident, or caused deliberately. After seeing them off, and instructing his builders to go home for the day, he turned to Jethro, Julian and David, and requested that they meet him in the library for a private chat. It didn't need an expert in body language to tell that something was seriously wrong with Jethro. David and Julian eyed each other nervously as he sat sobbing on the leather chesterfield. Percy placed a comforting arm around the gardener's shoulders, and came within a toucher of saying, 'There there!' which was rather noble of him, given what he'd recently witnessed and the kind of day he'd had.

"Oi never wanted to betray you," sobbed Jethro. "Oi've been blackmailed!"

Percy turned to Julian and David and explained. "When I came back to rescue the animals, I found Jethro here rifling through your drawers, Julian, presumably trying to steal money."

David looked sheepish. He'd recently borrowed one pound thirty-eight from the petty cash tin himself.

"No sir!" protested Jethro, in a scene reminiscent of 'The Wilmslow Boy'. "I wasn't stealing money. I may be a lot of things, but I'm not a thief. I was stealing the old key."

"What on earth would you want that for?" asked Julian, ignoring Jethro's shaky definition of theft.

"What key?" asked Percy, unabreast of recent developments.

"It's Lord Hickman, sir. He's out of prison, and he blackmailed me into doing it. Oi don't know why he wants it though."

"Hang on!" said David, shaken to the core. "Lord Hickman is out of prison you say?"

Jethro nodded. "He phoned me yesterday, and told me to steal the key with the 'H' on it."

Julian was confused. "But how could he ask you to steal a key when it was in the lake? We only found the bloody thing late last night."

"Ah sir," said Jethro. "He asked me to find it for him, and then, blow me down, if you didn't catch it with your fishin' rod, with the magnet on the end."

Now Percy was confused. "Why on earth did you go fishing with a magnet on the end of your line?"

"I had a game like that when I was a kid," added David. "You had a bowl full of metal fish, and a fishing rod with a magnet, and you...."

"I dropped my glasses in the lake," explained Julian, in an attempt to clarify the situation. "I was trying to look at a big carp, you see."

Percy was none the wiser. "But you have to keep your glasses on, Julian. They can't be thrown in to look at the carp for you. Glasses don't work like that."

Jethro continued. "It was fate, Mr Percy! Lord Hickman said I had to get him the 'H' shaped key, or he'd tell everybody about my secret, and I prayed to God to help me, because I was scared, and he sent me the key. It was a miracle."

"I see," said Percy, who plainly did not.

"But I can't live a lie no longer, Mr Percy. I've been thinking, and the best thing is to tell you everything. I want to get it off moi chest, but I'm afraid that you will all laugh at me."

"Of course we won't," Percy assured him, and re-introducing the arm around the shoulder. "Get it off your chest, son."

Jethro took a deep breath and began. "You see gents. For a long time now, Oi've felt strange. Oi looks loik a man, but I feels loik a woman."

"Don't we all!" whispered Julian, unhelpfully.

"What, like a woman trapped in a lady's body?" asked David, kicking the curator in the shin.

"That's roit!" replied Jethro, pleased that David, at least, was getting it. "I used to want to try women's clothes on, and when I did, they felt roit. I suppose you lads have noticed my hair's longer, and oi've been plucking moi eyebrows."

"Not really," lied Percy.

"Well, Lord Hickman knows about it, and he threatened to tell everybody unless I did what he said, but it broke moi heart to betray you all, 'cus you is all moi friends." He began to sob uncontrollably now. David patted his leg, and he continued.

"The trouble is, it's complicated. Oi feel attracted to men, but oi'm not a homo. It's because oi thinks like a woman. Oi'm in love with Glenda though, and she *is* a woman, but she's loik me and doesn't want to be a woman really."

“But I thought you *did* want to be a woman,” said Julian, puzzled.

“Shut up,” said Percy. “I’m following it, even if you’re not.”

“Glenda is in the same boat, see,” explained Jethro. “She feels loik a man trapped in a woman’s body, and she loves me too, but she’d rather oi was a woman, and she was a bloke, in an ideal world.”

“I’m going giddy,” frowned Julian, ruffling up his hair.

“And we wants to get married one day, but with Glenda as the man, and me as the woman. We both want to have surgery, but we can’t afford it.”

“I see,” said Percy, who appeared flustered. “Well, brushing that aside for a moment, this Lord Hickman can’t blackmail you any longer, not now it’s all out in the open, which is good news.”

“Yes, but it’s more complicated than that,” said Jethro. “It was Lord Hickman who burnt your stable block down to distract you while oi stole the key. Oi didn’t realize he’d go that far. He just said he’d cause a distraction.”

“Some bloody distraction,” sighed Julian. “My new box of cod steaks, all defrosted.”

Percy gave him one of his severe looks. “This old key must be bloody important, to warrant doing that. What could it possibly open? I’ve lived here for ages now, and never seen any keyholes that it would fit. Have you, Dave?”

David mulled it over. He knew Lord Hickman of old, and how his mind worked.

“There’s something valuable here, mark my words, and this key is the, er, well, the key. I vote we turn the old place upside down and unearth it. It may be a box, or a door, or even a secret compartment somewhere. If we all look, we’ll find it. Of course, it may well just be a key to another building altogether, in which case we have no chance, but you must admit, it's worth a go."

"I vote we tell the police, right away!" argued Percy. "This man is crazy, if he's willing to set fire to an historic house, just to cause a distraction, what will he do next?"

David wasn't so sure that Percy was right. "If you call the police, they might not find him, and if they did, they'd have a hard job proving for certain he'd done it. I know him, and he's slippery. He wants this key, and access to whatever it opens. It's my bet, knowing him as I do, that there's something here that he wants badly. Why not search the place now? If we fail, let Jethro give him the bloody key, and I bet he'll leave us alone."

Percy had to agree, though it rankled to be giving an arsonist and jailbird what he demanded in order to prevent him striking again. The four men decided to split up and go over the castle with a fine-toothed comb. If they'd found nothing by the end of the day, they agreed to use Jethro as a double agent. He would hand the key over, and hint that the castle was unoccupied on a certain evening. If the key *did* fit a keyhole in the building, surely Lord Hickman would choose that evening to strike, and Percy would ensure that he had a warm welcome prepared; namely, the boys in blue. If he didn't come, the key was almost certainly nothing to do with Stanmore Castle, and as such, nothing to concern them.

David chose to begin with the library and the exhibition rooms, whilst Julian took the sitting room and bedrooms. Percy and Jethro were responsible for the kitchens, the attic and anywhere else they could think of. By early evening, an exhaustive search had revealed absolutely nothing. They reconvened in the library for tea, all tired and dispirited except for Jethro, who confessed that it was far more exciting than carrying horse shit around in wheel barrows.

"Libraries should all be oak-lined like this one," said David, "and have secret panels, like in Agatha Christie books. I bet if you pull on that table lamp, the whole wall will slide across, like it used to do in 'The Man from Uncle.'

"Grow up," groaned Julian, somewhat uncharitably. He had, after all, just lost everything apart from what he was wearing, and that is bound to jade a person somewhat.

"Take all the books off the shelves," said David suddenly. "I've had an idea."

"Go and bollocks," replied Percy. "There's about ten thousand of them."

"I'll do it then," said David, "and I promise to put them all back." He began to clear whole shelves of their contents, stacking the books carefully on the parquet floor. He had all but given up after a complete wall, when suddenly he let out a whoop of delight.

Behind a sizeable book entitled 'Hans Holbein the Younger - His years at the court of Henry the Eighth' was a large brass keyhole, set into the oak panel. The key was duly fetched and inserted, whilst the library party held its breath. The key was badly rusted after lying in the lake, where it had been thrown by Lady Hickman on the day she vacated the castle, following her husband's imprisonment. She had no inkling as to the purpose of the key, just as she had no inkling about half of what her crooked, philandering husband got up to behind her back. She had discovered it in a box at the stables, along with a pile of steamy love letters from his various mistresses, and decided to drop it from her estranged husband's favourite bridge, as a final act of defiance, in the vain hope that one day, somehow, it would inconvenience him. She would have been deeply gratified to know that her stroppy final gesture had been successful in its aim, and amazed that someone would now be holding the very item again, after five long years amongst the carp.

David twisted the key gingerly. He didn't want it to snap in the keyhole with metal fatigue. He was also unsure whether the corroded 'H' shaped end was still up to the task. He needn't have worried. There was a satisfying clunk, and the panel became loose. He tried to slide it across, first to the left and then to the right, but the panel wasn't having any of it. Frustrated, he stood sipping tea, and looking for inspiration. They were so close, but as yet, there was no cigar.

Percy stepped up to the panel and studied it closely for a few seconds, before pushing it. It swung inwards to reveal a small dark room.

"Bloody artists!" he moaned. "It's a proper door on hinges, not a sliding panel, you turd!"

"There's gratitude for you!" moaned David, ashamed at his own stupidity.

Jethro was sent in search of a torch, and returned seconds later, beside himself with excitement. Percy selflessly suggested that his gardener should go in first, as the whole adventure had been inadvertently triggered by him. This he did, to the immense relief of David and Julian, who were still on edge from their recent encounters with The Undead.

"It's just a small room with a chest of drawers and a dusty old rug," announced Jethro. The others piled in behind him to see for themselves. It was, as Jethro had rightly stated, a room measuring no more than six by ten feet, simply plastered and painted a dirty green colour. There was a small, Persian-style rug and an old oak plan chest. Other than that and a musty smell, it was bare.

Percy knelt down by the chest, and asked Jethro to shine the light into the drawers as he opened them. The first one contained a ball of string, and the next three were empty, with the exception of the usual woodlouse corpses. The final drawer, however, contained a dusty artist's portfolio, tied with ribbon. Percy removed it and the four explorers returned to the library. David, in particular, was finding it hard to keep calm. He knew Lord Hickman's track record, and whatever was within the folder was unlikely to be a 'Paint by Numbers' tiger that he'd done himself. Percy carefully untied the ribbons and opened it. Inside was a folded piece of yellowed cartridge paper measuring approximately sixteen inches by twelve. There was not a sound as he examined it. It contained an exquisite terra-cotta coloured drawing of a small female child. She was around four years old, and dressed in what looked like Elizabethan or possibly Tudor clothing; the type worn by noble born families, rather than peasants. To the right of the girl's face were a name and a date, written in capital letters with a formal serif typeface. It said Jane Grey – 1542.

By now, all four men were clustered around the picture, straining to get a better view. David like the others, was enthralled by the quality of the drawing, but now another detail had diverted his attention. As he began to decipher the artist's small, insignificant signature, his jaw dropped.

"Oh my God!" he said suddenly. "Oh my God!"

Julian asked what the matter was.

"This is why Hickman needed that key," said David breathlessly. "Folks, you are almost certainly looking at a portrait of Lady Jane Grey as a child, by a man who knew a thing or two about painting royalty. This is a drawing by Hans Holbein the Younger – possibly one of the last drawings he ever did, judging by the date, and it could be worth millions, I repeat, millions, *if* it's real."

The discovery took a long time to sink in for three quarters of those present. Jethro, who hadn't the foggiest idea who Holbein was, seemed completely untroubled by it all, and simply reiterated that he was having a lovely time.

Glenda was summoned to provide more tea to calm their nerves, and Percy took the opportunity to inform her of the latest developments, vis-à-vis Hickman's failed blackmail plot. Jethro shuffled from foot to foot, and examined the pattern on the carpet, whilst she changed colour to something approaching vermilion. Sensing that the mood needed lightening, Julian raised his cup and wished them both a happy life together, to which Percy and David added 'here here!'

"I don't get it," said Percy. "If this is really a Holbein, David, how has this Hickman come by it, and how do you know it's Lady Jane Grey, rather than plain old Jane Grey from down the road?"

"Holbein was court painter to Henry the Eighth, and the superstar artist of his day," explained David. "Drawings like this would have usually have been preparatory sketches for a proposed oil painting, though not always. I'm not brilliant at art history, but I love Holbein's stuff, and I happen to know that he died the year after this, possibly in the plague of London. He was a German, but worked over here a lot, you see. Lady Jane Grey would have been his typical subject matter, coming from an aristocratic family, but the connection with Stanmore Castle is the real surprise. Did you know that she lived about a mile from here?"

"What, on the new estate?" asked Jethro, who felt that it high time he joined in with the conversation.

"Er, no Jeth," smiled David. "She lived at what is now The Whittington Inn down the road. It was built by the real Dick Whittington's grandfather, William de Whittenton in the year thirteen-ten, but the house passed to the Grey family much later than that, and Lady Jane briefly lived there, as a child. It's conceivable that Holbein drew her, and the portrait came to the house with the family, and stayed in the area, changing hands a few times of course. One thing's for certain. Whether Hickman found it locally or wasn't aware of the Kinver connection, I bet you any money he stole it."

"Maybe it was in the family," suggested the fair-minded Julian, acting as Lord Hickman's unofficial defence lawyer. "It could have been at the castle since Lord Henry Hickman's day, or even before."

"I doubt it," replied David, pushing out his bottom lip and shaking his head. "The man is a crook through and through. He acquired this illegally somehow, and he was saving it for a rainy day. I reckon he was figuring on asking me to fake it, once I'd proved I was trustworthy and I could do a good job on the other pictures. Unfortunately for him, he ended up in the nick before that could happen, and now he's come for it."

Julian was pacing the room now and messing with his hair, a sure sign that he was plotting something.

"Why don't you forge it now? If you could do it quickly, Jethro could hand him the key and give him the nod when we're all out, as was suggested, but with one important difference. We keep the Holbein, and he skedaddles with another of your excellent fakes!"

"By George, that's brilliant!" laughed Percy, slapping his curator on the back. "This Hickman doesn't know that we know about the secret room or the Holbein. He'd break in, steal the fake and disappear, and we'd be not only left in peace, but we'd have a real Holbein for the museum. That would fetch the punters in!"

"You're a genius, Jools," agreed David, with a devilish twinkle in his eye. "He'd then try to fence the painting to one of his bent art dealers, who would almost certainly know that it was a fake and probably punch his lights out."

"And the beauty of that…." interrupted Percy, excitedly, "…is he'd naturally presume that the picture in the secret room had always been a fake, meaning, of course, that he'd stolen a fake in the first place. He'd never suspect that his arch-enemy, David, was still here at the castle, and continuing to thwart him. He'll simply go away, and hopefully we won't be bothered by him again."

Julian was still deep in thought. "How long would it take you to copy the picture well enough to fool him?"

"Not long," said David confidently. "Luckily, it's a small terracotta drawing, rather than some grand oil painting. I'd have to get some heavy hand-made paper, tea-stain it to make it look old, and then start drawing. I could complete a small picture like that in a day, no problem."

"And it would look the business?"

"I'd challenge you to tell them apart," replied David smugly. "But remember, Lord Hickman won't have that choice. He'll see one Holbein, and presume it's the one he left in his drawer five years ago. It's perfect!"

## CHAPTER 9

## Third Time Lucky

"Tell me I didn't burn down a building for nothing?" asked Lord Hickman.

"You didn't burn down a building fer nothin'," replied Jethro.

"Good! Now tell me why the key isn't in the milk churn."

"Ah!" smiled Jethro, who had been going over his lines all day, and been thoroughly tested by Percy until he was satisfied. "I *knew* you'd ask me that. I knows exactly where the key is, Lord Hickman, but I was interrupted by the new owner, just as oi was about to steal it."

"Just as I interrupted you when you were trying my wife's dress on, you mean?"

Jethro's heart began to pound in his chest. He took deep breaths and continued.

"But oi've got a plan, sir, if you'll hear me out. Tomorrer noit, Percy, Julian and David is goin' to a show at the Town Hall called 'Jack the Ripper - the Musical', and they said they won't be back till midnoit. I can get your key then, and leave it in the milk churn before oi goes home."

"I see," said Lord Hickman. "Very well, but can I warn you that if my key isn't where it should be, the whole of the West

Midlands will know about Gardener's World's own version of Danny la Rue. Is that clear?"

"Yes sir."

"And one last thing. Does this castle have any vicious dogs or alarms?"

"Vicious dogs or alarms you say?" asked Jethro, floundering. He had not been primed to respond to this question. Percy the Prompt, standing beside him, shook his head violently. "No sir. There's a Labrador called Bertie, but you're more loikly to fall over him than get bitten, and the alarm is bust."

"Thank you, Jethro," said Lord Hickman. "And if you have lied to me, be assured that I will kill you, and it will be a horrible, slow death involving a pitchfork."

The phone went dead, and Percy patted his gardener on the back. "Well done old son. That was word perfect!"

Julian and David, who were eavesdropping outside the door, burst in and added their congratulations. David then returned to his room to concentrate on the Holbein, while Julian collared his boss, in order to discuss a topic that was causing him much unrest.

"Percy," he began falteringly. "It's about the ashabtis. As you know, I'm all for taking on new, exciting exhibits, but those things give me the creeps. Ever since they arrived, we've had a succession of creepy happenings. Adrian warned us about the curse, and he was right. This week alone, we've had a plague of locusts and a fire, and we all know that Lord Henry Hickman, his wife and butler disappeared, presumed crumbled to dust. Add to that a cat that regularly brings me severed digits, and I think you'll agree we have a slight problem."

Percy smiled a headmasterly smile, and gently recovered a stray pencil from his overwrought curator's hair.

"And all have perfectly logical explanations, Jools, I'm sure. For a start, we know what caused the fire, and it wasn't Rametup."

"That's not all," replied Julian hollowly. "A few nights ago, David and I were scared out of our wits by a mummy. This was no bad dream either. We were in bed, and David heard it coming up the stairs to get us."

Percy was beginning to think he was running a gay castle. "So you and David are, you know, like Jethro and Glenda?"

"No, no!" insisted Julian, emphatically. "We only slept in the same bed for protection."

"I must try that one on with Jane, the barmaid at the Fox Inn," laughed Percy. "Mind you, she did say to me recently that I couldn't sleep with her *without* protection, so I suppose it makes some sort of…."

"Look, to hell with Jane," snapped Julian, his nerves jangling. "We saw what we saw. This castle is haunted by a vengeful mummy, and I reckon it's trying to get its possessions back so that it can rest in peace, and I for one want to hand them over so that *I* can bloody well rest in peace."

Percy looked worried. After a few minutes of deep thought, he assured Julian that he could sling the ashabtis in the river if there was one more mummy sighting, and they'd have to go back to being the world's most boring museum. Julian, who was running the gamut of emotions from A to Z and back again, agreed to sleep on it, if indeed he could. Luckily, the office phone rang at that point, and diffused the situation a little. It was a rather high-powered lady with a London accent, asking for David Day.

David was duly summoned, and rushed to the receiver.

"David?" asked Lynette French. "Is that you? You said it would be okay to contact you on this number, so I hope you don't mind, sweetie. Look, I'll admit, I was a bit miffed with you after the

Tina Marina muddle, closely followed by the Frankfurt fiasco, but I've been reflecting, as one does, and I must admit that the first event wasn't your fault, and the second appears to have been an unfortunate series of freak occurrences. I just hope you're not one of these accident-prone types, dearie. Anyway, I've decided to give you one last chance, for the simple reason that your work is good. I have a job coming up, and Glynn Edwards, our long-standing caricaturist, can't do it."

"Thank you!"

"It's a pleasure sweetie, but let me down this time and it's definitely curtains, do you follow me?"

"Absolutely. Where is this job? Russia? Iceland maybe?"

"Cheeky bugger! It's in Birmingham City centre, which, if I recall, is fairly near to your house, is it not?"

David replied that it was indeed close to his house, unless of course she was referring to Birmingham, Alabama.

"Good," said Lynette, "The event is tomorrow night, at the Botanical Gardens, and it's a solicitor's black-tie dinner. You have to be there for seven, and draw from half-seven until ten-thirty. Can you do it?"

"Well, I did have tickets for 'Jack the Ripper - The Musical' at the Town Hall, but….."

"You can give that a miss. This is more important, sweetie," interrupted Lynette.

"That's what I was about to say," said David. "I'll be there."

"And remember," concluded Lynette, "last chance, so impress me, David. I'll be getting feedback from the senior partners, remember."

David assured her that he would pull out all the stops, and replaced the receiver.

Percy and Julian, who were still in the office, were quietly pleased. Since David's operation, he hadn't really had time to promote himself, and other than the poorly-paid museum work, he didn't really have too much on, work-wise. The Lynette French Agency was a big and influential outfit, and it paid to keep in with its boss. After his two consecutive disasters, this was an unexpected call, to say the least, and even though he had clearly been second choice, it was nevertheless welcomed. It was up to him to make amends now, and knock their socks off with some inspired cartooning. The only problem was, he felt he'd let his friends down a little.

"Good news!" smiled David, "But I'm afraid 'Jack the Ripper - The Musical' is off. You two will have to go without me."

Julian was first to speak. "Well Percy, I don't know how you feel, but personally, I'm broken-hearted. We spent ages inventing a totally bogus musical to go to, so that Lord Hickman could come into the castle and steal a forged Holbein, and now this bugger can't come with us to an event that doesn't exist anyway. I'm gutted; how about you?"

Percy roared with laughter and ruffled David's hair as he left the office. "Don't worry Davy Daydream, I find the fine line between fantasy and reality confusing too. I wouldn't worry about it!"

"Shit!" sighed David, turning cerise with shame. "I'm always doing that! I think that's why I'm such a good liar. I actually *believe* what I'm telling people!" He scurried off to continue work on his Holbein, deeply concerned for his own sanity.

* * *

David pulled onto the car park of Birmingham's Botanical Gardens and turned off the ignition. He turned the rear-view mirror towards him and adjusted his black bow-tie. It was his first time behind the wheel since the operation, and it felt good to be mobile again. Recent brushes with public transport, he felt, had not been an overwhelming success, and his track record, so to speak, vis-à-vis the huge gulf between his desired and actual destinations was not good. Tonight, he was rather pleased with himself. He had found the Botanical Gardens first time, with no wrong turns or swearing, and his groin had held up splendidly, with no pliers attacks to report in over three days. Life was on the up, and about time too.

He opened the boot, pulled out his caricaturist's kit and his fold-up stool, and walked through the automatic glass doors into the cloakrooms. He continued through into the first of the hot houses, which was, he thought, rather wonderful. There was a tiled floor, with a raised fishpond and water fountain in the middle, and all manner of exotic plants and giant palm trees surrounding it, basking in the hot, wet air. The elaborate glass and metal roof was of Victorian construction, and through it, David could see the night sky, and a million twinkling stars.

A man's voice called out, "How you doin'?"

This took David by surprise. "Very well thank you!" he replied, hoping to God the question had been aimed at him. It was difficult to tell, as he couldn't see anyone else in the room, due to the dense tropical foliage.

The man's voice spoke once more. "Are you lost, mate?"

"Not exactly," replied David, "But if you could show me which room the solicitor's dinner is in, I'd be grateful."

There was silence.

"Hello?" called David. "Where are you?"

"F*** off, shit face!" replied the voice.

This was perplexing. The Botanical Gardens was supposed to be a sophisticated place. Obviously the venue was going downhill fast. He made a mental note to write to the management in the near future. For the time being, at least, he was far more concerned with getting out alive. Somehow, in this dense rainforest, he had unwittingly made an enemy. Perhaps it was one of those Japanese soldiers who thought the war was still going on, thirty years later. The Daily Mail often reported such stories, and they would not fabricate these things. He edged around the perimeter, desperate to get out of the dark, lonely and frightening jungle he found himself in.

The voice spoke again, giving David the fright of his life. It appeared to be right behind him now, but at least his antagonist's tone had lightened.

"How's your mother?"

He turned quickly to confront his stalker. It was a Mynah bird called Jim - it said so on his cage. David swallowed deeply and continued his way around the wall, ashamed of his foolishness. The voice spoke once more.

"Are you lost, mate?"

David decided to teach the evil creature a new expletive or two. "Go and shag yourself, you evil black bastard."

Winston Roberts, the Jamaican events manager, was not used to being spoken to this way, and he made David aware of the fact in no uncertain terms. After ten minutes of furious back-pedalling, embarrassed explanation, sycophantic grovelling and a blow-by-blow account of David's impeccable history of race relations, the two men agreed to begin again. Winston, who could now see the funny side, pointed David in the direction of the larger function room. As he scurried off down the steps, he heard Winston shout, "Bugger off out of here, you shitty white bastard!"

David had presumed that his and the events manager's differences had been cleared up amicably, and was somewhat taken aback. He back-tracked to where Winston was standing, staring up at the night sky, giggling to himself in a deranged way.

"There was no need for that!" complained David, disappointed. Winston just continued to giggle, and pointed at a white dove, sat high up on the ornamental ironwork. He then brought to David's attention the revolting twelve-inch streak of bird diarrhoea striping the back of his brand new dinner suit. After a brief diversion to the toilets in reception, David once more strutted through the hot house and past his one-time adversary. Winston, who, like David, was prone to uncontrollable giggling fits, turned away, bit his sizable lip and began to study a particularly interesting cactus.

The reception room was alive with activity. Smartly dressed waiters wearing white merchant navy-style jackets with gold epaulettes were pouring row after row of champagnes, Bucks Fizzes and orange juices, and arranging them on a linen-covered trestle table near the entrance. In the adjoining dining room, waitresses busied themselves adding finishing touches to the tables, while the band sound-checked on stage. David found himself a little corner, arranged two comfy chairs and a small coffee table, and prepared his drawing paper and clipboard. This was the nervous time, before the guests arrived. He paced the room liked a caged tiger for half an hour, until the first people began to slowly trickle in.

Once the crowd had swelled to around fifteen, he decided to introduce himself. Luckily, the first person he spoke to was a gregarious, rotund little man with a great face for caricature, and after five minutes of intense drawing, victim number one emerged from Cartoonist's Corner, declaring his drawing a success, and recommending it to all and sundry. Quite soon David had got himself a queue, and the room was buzzing with dinner-suited gents and ladies in posh frocks. After an hour in the drinks reception, the guests were called into dinner, and David dutifully followed with his fold-up stool. He then began to draw in-situ around the tables, watched from afar by Winston, who was sporting a massive toothy smile.

During a convenient lull in the proceedings, he popped over and advised David to concentrate on the top table, where all the V.I.P.s were seated, arguing that it would be they who would be responsible for any re-bookings that might result from a good performance. Thanking him for the advice, David began to draw the directors of the company, to universal applause, and rounded off one of the most consistent and 'on form' evenings that he'd had for a long time, with a wonderful, if slightly uncharitable, cartoon of the company's chairman.

"Well, what a nice surprise. You've been marvellous!" he beamed, slipping David a ten pound note. "I hope we have fed you and treated you well, and it was lovely to see how most of my staff members were willing to be drawn! We accountants often get accused of being boring and po-faced, but it's really not true you know!"

David had to concur. They had been a lovely, appreciative crowd, and he had enjoyed the evening. The chairman requested a business card, but David explained that it was Lynette Franks who had booked him, and it was only right that any future bookings should go through her. He said goodnight to Winston and everyone on the chairman's table, packed away his pens and paper, and walked back through the hot house. The heady scent of tropical flowers, coupled with the sense of elation he always felt after a successful evening, made him feel almost intoxicated. He bade a cheery two-fingered farewell to Jim the Mynah bird, and skipped into the reception and cloak room areas.

Thinking it wise to relieve himself before driving back to Stourbridge, he laid down his attaché case and stool next to the free-standing polished brass notice board, which the Botanical Gardens used to officially welcome guests.

Something buried deep within his brain flashed to the forefront and then promptly disappeared, as quickly as a startled gazelle. It left him feeling vaguely uneasy, as if he'd had a disconcerting dream, but could no longer remember it. For some reason, something began to trouble him, but he was damned if he could work out what it was. He wandered into the toilets and stood against the trough, deep in thought.

It was then that it hit him. He felt sick to the pit of his stomach now, and the room was swimming. He staggered out to his car and drove home in a silence that was punctuated only by the occasional expletive-ridden outbursts – mostly comprising of words that would have made even Jim the Mynah bird blush.

## CHAPTER 10

## The Return of the Fat Man.

When old acquaintances meet up after many years apart, there is usually a lot of back-slapping, hand-shaking and general good natured bonhomie. Anecdotes fly around, and are greeted by warm laughter and occasionally even a few poignant tears.

This particular re-union had none of the above.

Herr Grunstrasse, a fat, sixty-something German in a crumpled cream linen suit, sat with his pilot Pierre in his four-seater light aircraft on the tarmac of Twopenny Green Aerodrome, Tutton Common, near Kinver. One of the two back seats was occupied by Lord Hickman, who was clutching a dusty old artist's portfolio.

There was no love lost between these gentlemen, and with good cause. The last time they had met was five years before, in exactly the same aerodrome, and exactly the same spot. Lord Hickman, believing that he was the proud owner of a Monet and a Botticelli, was endeavouring to sell them to Herr Grunstrasse, blissfully unaware that David Day had switched them for his own expert forgeries, and was intending to return the originals to their rightful owner.

The German art dealer, who knew more than a little about spotting fakes from a mile away, became understandably miffed about being dragged across Europe on a wild goose chase to look at two paintings that weren't even properly dry yet, and instructed his pilot, Pierre, to ventilate the crooked aristocrat with his Walther automatic until he resembled a colander. Luckily for Lord Hickman - if one can call it lucky - David Day and his friend Mo, (who was built very much along the lines of a brick-built public convenience, and was slightly musclier than a leather chesterfield settee) less than ably assisted by constables Donald and Pongo, intervened, resulting in all three serving lengthy jail sentences.

Herr Grunstrasse, unlike his English co-conspirator, had been a free man for over a year, but the memory of that encounter was still green, (or 'Grun' as he pronounced it) and his first reaction, upon receiving a call from his old adversary, Lord Hickman, was to tell him to shove his head into the rectal cavity of a large polar bear. His rather harsh and unforgiving stance melted somewhat, however, on hearing that a genuine Holbein drawing was on offer. The German's opening gambit, upon greeting his old enemy, had been predictable.

"Who the hell are you? You speak like Hickman, but you are not the Lord Hickman I remember."

"Ah yes!" smiled the small, blond gentleman in the back seat. "What do you think? I felt I needed a new start, and a new face to match."

"The effect for me is similar to gilding a rotten potato," sneered the fat man. "Show me the picture."

Lord Hickman handed the folder to Pierre, who handed it to his boss. Small beads of sweat formed on Herr Grunstrasse's huge brow as he opened the folder and studied the drawing carefully. He took out a small folding magnifying glass and ran a beady eye over the picture at close quarters, after mopping his brow to avoid potential accidents. He turned his face towards Lord Hickman, who was sitting nervously in the back seat, awaiting judgment. It was purple, and like thunder – the face, not the seat.

"Who do you think I am, you stupid, English upper-crust bastard?" he growled. "Do you think I was born yesterday afternoon?"

Lord Hickman's jaw dropped. He knew full well what the German was about to insinuate, and he didn't like it one bit. The provenance of that drawing was impeccable, and no fat, sweaty art dealer was going to tell him otherwise.

"If you think you can pull that stunt on me," fumed the wounded aristocrat, "You can think again. I admit that you were shown forgeries last time, and you know full well that I was duped by David Day, as we all were. Now you are trying to pull the wool over my eyes, and rob me of a real Holbein. Do you really think I'm that naïve?"

Herr Grunstrasse was apoplectic now. "*You* are the naïve one, you ignorant swine, if you genuinely believe this to be real. Look! Tea-stained paper. Can you see this tiny watermark on the back? You can buy this brand of paper from art stores, and look here, next to the watermark. Whoever faked it forgot to remove the price. It's written in faint pencil; thirty-five pence! I think you will find that decimalization didn't exist in the fifteen-forties, unless I'm very much mistaken."

Lord Hickman was reeling now. He had been made to feel utterly foolish, and it was beginning to dawn on him who was responsible. David Day was at the castle; he'd seen him with his own eyes. Somehow, he must have discovered that the old key opened the hidden room. Hickman had let his guard down and fallen for their subterfuge. The key, Jethro's hint that they'd all be out at the theatre – it was all a set up, and he'd swallowed it hook, line and sinker. He could see David Day's hand all over this. The real Holbein was still at the castle; he was convinced of it, and now the kid gloves were coming off. He needed the money, and nobody was going to get in his way. He braced himself, and addressed the German. This was going to have to be good, or his one chance of selling the picture and setting himself up with enough money to begin his new life was going to disappear in a puff of smoke."

"Herr Grunstrasse, I want you to listen very carefully," he began. "When we last met, I really did own a genuine Monet, and also a Botticelli. You know that now, I hope. That little bastard art student who shopped us both to the police switched the pictures, so that I would look ridiculous in front of you, an internationally acclaimed art dealer."

Herr Grunstrasse liked this so far. Food, and a susceptibility to flattery were his only weaknesses. Lord Hickman continued.

"The Holbein *was* genuine. I have the provenance. The drawing was found in an old chest of drawers at The Whittington Inn two hundred and fifty years ago by a Mr Follett, a local industrialist and patron of the arts. He read up on the picture, and the house, and put two and two together. Lady Jane Grey lived at the house as a child. Holbein mentioned a drawing of the four-year-old Jane Grey in his diaries; it was one of the last pieces he drew, before succumbing to the plague in London, but until then, no one knew what had become of the picture. Mr Follett kept it at his mansion near Stourbridge, and when he died, it was passed down to the family. Unfortunately, as so often happens, the man's descendants were philistines, and had no idea what they had in their attic. One evening, just before I was incarcerated, I had dinner with the current Mr Follett, a Black Country industrialist and social climber who understood nuts and bolts and galvanized buckets, but precious little else. After he'd swallowed a bottle of vintage port and bored me to death with his dreary golfing anecdotes, he asked my advice on the contents an old suitcase full of pictures and letters, as he was having a clearout. He had no idea what the drawing was, and told me he didn't want 'dowdy old rubbish' in his house, which, typical of the Nouveau Riche cretins of this area, was full of awful Russell Flint limited edition prints of naked Spanish women. I spotted the quality of the drawing straightaway, but kept calm. I don't think he'd read the old letters of provenance, but even if he had, it would have meant nothing to him. Of course, I simply couldn't allow such a moron to own an important picture like that, so I persuaded him to drink another glass of port, laced with one of my own ingredients, and took the drawing and the letters of provenance as he lay comatose in his armchair. The next day he phoned to tell me what a dreadful hangover he'd got, and to this day he hasn't even realized his bloody things were missing! These moronic working-class people who make a few quid and think it buys them breeding and sophistication. They hang onto their crap and give away their treasures."

Herr Grunstrasse eyed him critically. "But not you eh, Lord Hickman? You try to sell your crap and hang onto your treasures, don't you?"

Lord Hickman objected in the strongest possible terms. "Both times I have acted in good faith and been cheated by David Day. I have discovered that he is now living, or at least working, at the castle. It is obvious what has happened here. He is up to his old tricks again, but this time he will regret it. The Holbein is still at the castle; I would stake my life on it, and I intend to get back what is rightfully mine. I ask you to be patient, Herr Grunstrasse. I will pay for you and Pierre to stay at The Fox Inn for the night. I guarantee that the real Holbein will be handed over by tomorrow evening, and you'll be back in the fatherland by midnight. What do you say?"

"I'll give you till tomorrow afternoon - five o'clock," replied the German. "Then we fly home."

Lord Hickman thanked him brokenly and headed across country to his rural retreat. As he walked through the farmer's field with a determined stride, he felt inside his suit jacket. The warm, wooden handle of his Smith and Wesson made him feel infinitely more confident about what was ahead. He had never been one to carry firearms, unlike some of his baser acquaintances, but the meeting with Herr Grunstrasse had given him cause for concern. During their previous, ill-fated encounter, things had turned a little nasty when the art dealer discovered that the paintings were fakes, and his creepy little Dutch pilot, Pierre van der Truck, had begun to wave a Walther around, providing an excellent, if unexpected cure for the Lord's constipated bowel. Though it rankled, this time it was important to have some form of self-defence, just in case history repeated itself.

Now the Smith and Wesson could be used to extract a Holbein original from the castle, and if David Day accidentally got a bullet in the arse, so much the better.

* * *

"You'll be pleased to know that the forensics boys have finally got their fingers out," announced Constable Donald Bates to his captive audience, namely Julian and David. He had been working on this pun for most of the drive from Kinver to the castle grounds, and he was obviously very proud of it, but also a little disappointed that his colleague, Constable Pongo had slept through his finest comedy moment.

"The good news is that the fingers have been dead for a long time. The boffins are only just beginning their series of tests, as you'll appreciate, but they have already made one very important discovery. The fingers were treated with some form of embalming fluid. That's why they are in such good condition. Also, the types of marks they found indicate that the fingers may possibly have been wrapped in bandage at some point."

Julian slumped into his chair and began to ruffle his hair furiously, freeing up a 2B pencil stub that had been missing for several weeks.

"That's it! I knew it. We are all cursed. Those blasted ashabtis are going in the canal."

The telephone rang, causing the nervous curator to leap out of his chair like a rocketing pheasant. It was a lady with a posh London accent asking for David, who had now, like Julian, drained of colour. David desperately began to mouth the word 'No' whilst waving frantically with both hands. Being astute, and sensing that there was some underlying message in the young artist's body language, Julian asked the lady if it was possible to try again in five minutes, as the person she needed to speak to was being spoken to by the police. At this juncture, Percy popped his head around the door and informed the officer that Glenda had prepared a plate of sandwiches and a pot of tea in the library. Donald, who was rather embarrassed that Pongo had asked in the first place, gently woke the sleeping policeman, and the two made their way along the corridor, leaving Julian and David alone with their thoughts, which, though different in subject matter, were equally taxing.

"As I was trying to explain, before the coppers arrived," continued David, "I am in shit creek without a paddle, and I need your help with a good excuse. I'd just finished work at the Botanical Gardens, and I was on top of the world, when I decided to go for a piss. I dropped my gear down by this brass sign thingy; you know the ones, where the venue can put stick-on letters onto the board to welcome visitors. So I read this sign, and it said;

*The Botanical Gardens welcomes;*

*Heathcotes Solicitors Annual Dinner – The Terrace Suite.*

*Bogel Brookes Huey Accountants. Summer Ball – The Garden Suite.*

And then this horrible, sick feeling came over me. I'd been drawing in the wrong bloody room. Lynette told me they were solicitors, and I always get confused with solicitors and accountants.

“They’re completely different,” explained Julian helpfully. “Solicitors are boring bastards, but Accountants are *really* boring bastards.”

“Yes, hilarious!” sighed David. “Now I’m about to get a phone call from this woman which will go down in the annals of history as the most cringe-making, embarrassing bollocking ever, and right now I just want the earth to open up and swallow me whole.”

The phone rang.

David slumped into his chair with his head in his hands, and took the receiver from Julian.

“Ah, David,” said Lynette. “I’ve phoned to thank you.”

David winced and braced himself for the onslaught.

“When they told you that the Heathcote’s coach had broken down in Warwick, you could easily have gone home, satisfied that you had fulfilled your part of the bargain, and demanded payment, but you didn’t. I think it was incredibly sweet of you to offer your services to the dinner going on in the other room, rather than take the money and run. I don’t know another artist who would have done that. Anyway, your kind gesture paid real dividends, and I want to thank you! I’ve just had a call from Mr Bogel, who is the chairman of Bogel Brookes Huey. We’ve been courting them for ages and never got anywhere. He said you told him that Lynette French had arranged a caricaturist as a surprise for their Summer Ball, and he was so impressed by our initiative that he’s asked for a meeting about handling their P.R. work. I shall be sending you a couple of bottles of Champagne along with your cheque, and thank you very much from all of us here.”

David resembled an explorer who had been shot in the back of a neck by with a paralysis dart by a passing pygmy. It took a huge effort to reply, and when he eventually did, it felt as if he was speaking in slow motion.

“Thank you Lynette. It was the least I could do, after the first two disasters.”

“I have erased them from my memory, sweetie!” chirped Lynette. “If we land Bogel Brookes Huey, it’ll be more than worth it.” And with that, she was gone.

David now had a grin on his stupid face that would need to be surgically removed, but Julian’s mood had not lightened. He was about to moot his proposal to sling both ashabtis in the Staffs and Worcs Canal, when Percy appeared once more, looking flushed.

“Sorry to interrupt,” he began, “but Glenda just answered the door to a little man with a Brummie accent who claimed he was the Museum’s Inspector for the West Midlands. She invited him in, shoved him in the storeroom and locked the door. He’s going ballistic, so we might need some assistance.”

David and Julian ran down the corridor and into the hall, where the door of the storeroom was in imminent danger of coming off its hinges.

“You don’t think, for one minute, there *is* a West Midlands Museums Inspector do you?” asked David.

“Well I’ve never heard of one,” replied the curator, “though I must admit, our track record with regard to storeroom incarceration is somewhat mixed.”

Percy, who was looking agitated, remembered that he was entertaining guests, and scurried off to the library.

The voice within the storeroom bellowed its protest.

“My name is Reginald Bills, and I am a Museum Inspector. Now will you kindly let me out of this cupboard? I have never been treated like this before, and I have visited museums the length and breadth of the country. If you think, after this disgusting display of bad manners, that you will be awarded any stars whatsoever in the new Government ratings, you will have to think again!”

Julian gulped as if he'd swallowed a football and stared helplessly at David, as if imploring him to offer guidance. David stepped forward and unlocked the door, dropping back smartly to line up with his friend, in order to perfect their synchronized grovelling display. For a few seconds, nothing happened. Then, slowly, the door knob turned, the door pushed open, and a small, blond-haired man stepped blinking into the light.

"Ah, thank you, gentlemen," he smiled, dusting himself off and adjusting his tie. He produced a large Smith and Wesson revolver from his inside jacket pocket, and pointed it at them.

"Nice to see you again, Mr Day. I recognized you right away, but you obviously didn't recognize me. I've been through a few cosmetic changes since we last met, but I'm pleased to say, the revolting Birmingham accent was only ever intended to be temporary, unlike yours. Now would you kindly lead me to the real Holbein? I'd hate to have to cause any un-necessary leaks in that nasty, undernourished body of yours."

With less than perfect timing, Percy, Donald and Pongo arrived in the hall, to be greeted by the barrel of a gun that looked as if it could quite easily fell an elephant.

"Ah, Mr Payne!" said Lord Hickman. "The new owner! I'm so sorry, but we haven't been formally introduced. I'm Lord Charles Hickman, the previous and rightful owner. My family have lived in this castle for hundreds of years, but don't feel guilty. It wasn't your fault. It was this little shit's fault actually, wasn't it David? Oh my goodness, what on earth is that smell? You really should attend to the drainage, Mr Payne. The place is falling into wrack and ruin!"

Pongo's physical reaction to the revolver was understandable, if unfortunate. His colleague, Donald, addressed the intruder, sensing that his partner was otherwise engaged and looking a bit flustered.

"Look sir, I don't know who you are, or why you're waving that gun around, but if anyone gets shot, you'll be looking at a long prison sentence. Place the gun on the floor and we can talk about it."

"Ah, *now* I recognize you!" sneered Lord Hickman. "It's the very same pair of cretinous coppers that arrested me five years ago at the aerodrome. Well I never! The three musketeers, all together again, and who's this character with the pencil in his hair? D'Artagnan? Now listen. I'm going to aim this gun at Mr Day over there, and in one minute's time, I'm going to plant a little piece of lead into the cavity where his brain should be, unless someone here fetches me an original Holbein drawing; how's that?"

Julian raised his hand. "Lord Hickman, don't do anything silly. I know where the picture is. I'll get it, okay?"

"I knew you would," he smiled. "Trot along now. One minute, there's a good chap."

Julian hurtled down the corridor to his office and returned, breathless, a few seconds later with the folder.

"Show it to me!" ordered Lord Hickman. Julian opened the folder with trembling hands and showed him the drawing.

"Keep the bloody thing still," he shouted. "I need to make sure this isn't more subterfuge. I wouldn't put it past this bastard to forge several copies, just to confuse everyone - he's done it before. Good! Now close the folder and hand it to me slowly. One false move and I'll supply you with a neat little hole in *your* head to keep your pencil in."

Julian began to perspire like a glass-blower's backside as he handed over the folder. Lord Hickman glared at his attentive audience and swept his gun from left to right.

"Right gentlemen. I now intend to walk out of here without interference from any of you. You will give me five minutes to make my escape, and then you are free to go about your business. Do I make myself clear?"

"Transparently so!" replied Percy. "The invisible man could not be clearer."

Lord Hickman backed up to the front door. He slipped the folder under his arm and opened the door with his left hand, whilst aiming the gun provocatively at David's head. He quickly backed out of the door and slammed it behind him. One second later, there was an almighty crashing sound, accompanied by a scream, a thud, and then silence. Donald dashed to the door, and with an admirable mix of bravery and foolhardiness, yanked it open to reveal the prostrate and unconscious body of Lord Hickman on the stone steps. He was lying face up, with his legs still hooked around the sleeping twelve stone body of Bertie the Labrador. Three feet further on, and slightly to the right, was a Smith and Wesson revolver, and ditto, but slightly to the left, the old art folder. Donald and Pongo lifted the comatose aristocrat's head in order to establish the official cause of his unconsciousness, and discovered a lump at the back of his head the size, consistency and colour of a cricket ball. Donald applied the handcuffs, whilst David retrieved the drawing and Pongo retrieved the gun. Julian and Percy, meanwhile, tended to Bertie, showering him with well-earned praise.

"This deserves a celebration!" declared Percy, as the panda car eventually powered out of the drive. "Round up Jethro and Glenda, and we'll go to The Fox."

Two hours later, after a good dinner, a few pints and a lot of celebratory banter, Percy asked for the bill. David, meanwhile, full to the plimsoll line with Tutton Ale, decided to pay a quick visit to the lavatory. Never one to display his negligible manhood in public, he chose the privacy of a cubicle, and was surprised to hear a German voice conversing with what he guessed was a Netherlands one. Though similar when speaking English, he could discern the subtle differences, thanks to the occasional caricaturing job at foreign trade shows. The combination of German *and* the Netherlands sent a shiver down his spine. He was frantically putting two and two together in his head, and the result, for once, was four. This was Herr Grunstrasse, or David was a Dutchman. He held his breath and tried to eavesdrop on their conversation. The German seemed to be insinuating that five o'clock was as long as he was prepared to wait, while his colleague favoured leaving immediately. After a few terse words, the German asserted his authority, and the two agreed that they would be ready to set off bang on five. The rest of the conversation was obscured by the sound of the hot air hand drier, which, in spite of its inability to dry anyone's hands, appeared to have been powered by a Rolls Royce jet engine.

When the coast was clear, David dashed back to the pub's little back room with his head down, and told his colleagues what he had witnessed.

"These characters are ruthless," he concluded. "The last time we met, the little swivel-eyed Dutchman pulled a gun on us, and I wouldn't mind betting he's got one today. They're here to buy what is probably a stolen work of art, and I think we should stop them leaving until Donald and Pongo have had a word, don't you?"

"Oh right!" nodded Julian. "The Dutch bloke's got a gun too. Every other chap in South Staffordshire's got one today. Never mind, let's confront them, eh?"

"I'm not *that* daft," David assured him. "I think I'll pop back to the castle to pick up some of my equipment, and we'll visit the aerodrome for ten minutes, before they show up. Meanwhile, do me a favour, Percy, and ring the cops for me. Ask them to be waiting from four onwards, just in case, and it might be an idea to bring the artillery. If Donald and Pongo don't get promoted after this, there's no justice."

* * *

David and Julian walked unsteadily back to the castle along the bridle path, feeling like a pair of eleven-year-olds. Neither was used to drinking at lunchtimes, and it had gone straight to their heads. If David had been able to whistle, he would have been trilling a jaunty tune. A casual observer with poor eyesight would have mistaken them for Oliver Hardy and Charlie Chaplin, as both were sporting small, black moustaches and wearing dungarees. David was carrying a large tin of blackboard paint while Julian carried two four-inch emulsion brushes.

"How long does it take to dry?" asked Julian, struggling to prevent another giggling fit.

"It's rock hard in about an hour," replied David. "They'll never get it off the windscreen."

"I hope we did the right plane," said Julian, panicking a little. "We could be done for delicious mamage."

"Don't worry!" he was assured. "It's the same one they had five years ago. It's ingrained on my mind!"

A Wood Pigeon called in a nearby copse, a sound that David always found deeply sentimental.

"I reckon these wood pigeons have added an extra syllable to their call since I was a kid. It's probably to bring them into line with Europe. When we had a little caravan in Tenbury Wells, my granddad used to tell me that the birds were saying, 'Hello, David!' Now they seem to be saying, 'Hello there, David!'"

Julian looked at him askance. "You know my friend; I would love to see what goes on inside your mind."

David added a pair of crude eyebrows to his comrade's face with his emulsion brush, changing the effect from Oliver Hardy to Groucho Marx in one fell swoop.

They were nearing the museum now, when they spotted a kindred spirit. It was Hitlerina, another moustachioed castle-dweller, and she was prowling around by the large garden wall that separated the private grounds of Stanmore Castle from the adjoining farmer's field. Julian whispered that they should observe her for a few minutes, in the hope that she would perhaps lead them to where she had been finding her grisly body parts. After fifteen minutes of crouching in the undergrowth, David Attenborough-style, feeling ever-so-slightly ridiculous with their painted-on moustaches and being bitten senseless by a swarm of aggressive gnats, David decided that enough was enough, and was just about to try and persuade his locked knees to stand up, when Hitlerina suddenly disappeared down a small hole by the wall, in a fashion popularized by white rabbits.

David and Julian ran over to the perimeter wall and stood waiting at the hole, which was no more than eight inches across. Their patience was finally rewarded, some five minutes later, when Hitlerina emerged, covered in dust and cobwebs. There is no fooling a cat, generally speaking, and they are markedly less gullible than their canine counterparts when it comes to recognizing the human beings in their life. A dog, when confronted by its owner wearing a new moustache, is prone to bark dementedly, or run for cover behind the settee, depending on temperament, whereas the average cat coolly assesses the situation, and quickly realizes that the changes, whilst unflattering, are not a threat. After a short period of calm reflection, Hitlerina strolled nonchalantly over to her heavily-disguised master and presented him with the fruits of her latest expedition. It is always tricky for a cat to know what to get for the educated young man who has everything he needs, but she had chosen wisely.

It was a withered thumb.

## CHAPTER 11

## Hitlerina's Bunker

Percy was at a loss. As far as he knew, the hole didn't go anywhere. He tried to poke a stick down it, an action which seemed to completely unnerve Julian, but this served little purpose, other than to show that the tunnel seemed to be going under the wall and back into the courtyard. A torch was brought, but the tunnel turned sharply after a few feet, so the results were disappointing. Other than calling in the diggers and tearing up the cobbled yard, there was nothing he could do.

"I wonder if the house is built on an old graveyard or something," mused Julian. "Perhaps this bit of subsidence leads to a crypt of some kind."

"Well, if there is a crypt or a tunnel," replied Percy, "I reckon, judging by the angle of the hole, it's in between the library and this wall."

"These old houses had priest holes," David reminded them. "The Whittington Inn has one, and they reckon at one time, there was a tunnel that led all the way to Whittington Hall. When priests were being persecuted, they could pop up like rabbits hundreds of yards away and bugger off, rather than hanging around in a priest hole, waiting to be caught. These tunnels were useful for other things too, like in the civil war, if the cavaliers needed to disappear quickly when the roundheads arrived."

Julian concurred. "The place is certainly old enough to have had a tunnel or a priest hole, Percy. Any idea where it could have been?"

The thought had crossed Percy's mind, but old plans of the house didn't show anything, and the previous owner, in fairness, had not had the opportunity to fill him in on the interesting historical features, due to a pressing engagement.

"I can't imagine we've missed anything," he concluded. "We ransacked the place when we found the secret room, remember."

David had developed a faraway look in his eye, and was holding his jaw with his right hand in a thoughtful manner.

"What if the secret room has a secret room?"

"What?" asked Julian.

"The secret room! The best place to hide a secret room is in another secret room, don't you think? If you discovered the first one, you'd naturally think you'd cracked it, job done, and retire from secret room-finding activities, unaware that another one was lurking within it, like those Russian dolls you see in gift shops. It's worth a look, don't you think?"

"Of course!" agreed Percy, "But I can't honestly say that I hold much hope, old son."

They scampered back into the library, crossing their fingers that Lord Hickman had left the old key behind when he stole the faked Holbein. Luckily, it was still in the door panel, just as the books were still all over the floor where he had strewn them. Percy made a mental note to hire a cleaner, if and when the museum began to pick up a little.

The interior of the secret room was as they had left it. David began to melodramatically tap the walls, but they were all of solid construction. He took up the old Persian rug and examined the quarry tiles, but they too were permanent features. Julian and Percy, meanwhile, shoved the old plan chest to one side, but all they found beneath were more quarry tiles. Julian bent down to examine the tiles more closely, and began to scratch away the grout with his fingernails.

"This may be something or nothing," he frowned. "Look here! All the tiles have a good half inch of grout around them, but in this section, there's a hairline crack and it runs around in a square. You'd hardly notice if you weren't looking for it. The trouble is, I can't get any purchase on it to lift it up. There's nothing to get my fingers into."

Percy disappeared and came back seconds later with a large sink plunger and a twelve-inch steel rule. "Try this!" he suggested. "If that doesn't work, slip the rule into the grout and lever it up."

Julian chose the plunger. He spat on it to give it extra suction, rammed it down into the centre of the tiled area and pulled. A two-foot square section of tiles, mounted on a thick, oak board, came away from the rest of the floor. Beneath was a set of roughly hewn oak steps, leading into a pitch-black chasm.

For a whole minute, the three stared blankly at each other. Finally, Percy spoke.

"Who's first down?"

"Me," said Julian.

"My ventriloquism lessons really paid off!" laughed David. "Seriously though. Did I just hear you properly?"

"I was being jocular!" replied Julian. "I'm not going down there; not after what Hitlerina keeps finding for us. I think Jethro should go. I'll go get him."

"I should go first," said Percy, mulling things over. "It is my house, after all."

"Good man!" said David. "I'll follow you then. Here's the torch."

“I’ll stand guard here then,” added Julian bravely.

Percy climbed slowly into the abyss, his heart in his mouth. There is something about the thought of descending a ladder into a freezing cold, black tunnel full of zombies that has a certain effect on a fellow, though the effect can be markedly different according to the individual. Some experience a tingling sensation on the back of their necks, whilst others note a quickening of the heart. With Percy, it felt as if his bowels had tied themselves into the Staffordshire knot, prior to starting work on the reef, sheep-shank, hitch, slip and Windsor. Some days, it felt as if he had bitten off more than he could chew with Stanmore Castle. If he was honest, it was most days.

He arrived safely at the bottom and called up to David.

“It’s about ten feet deep, and there’s a corridor of sorts, heading out across the courtyard, as we suspected. It seems to have been hewn out of the sandstone, and there’s filthy straw on the floor, and, oh shit, there are rats!”

“I’m coming down,” replied David, amazed at his own bravery. “I’m okay with rodents. I owned a hamster as a child. As long as I have your word that there are no fat moths, I’ll be fine.”

They fumbled their way along the tunnel, nervously shining the torch this way and that, and jumping several feet into the air each time a rat swaggered past. After around fifteen yards, their progress was halted by a crudely-laid stone wall, with some distinctly amateurish mortar-work.

“Well, that’s it!” frowned Percy. “We can’t go any further. Whatever this once was, it looks as if it was bricked up years ago.”

David was not about to give up, after he had got this far. “Come on Perce,” he pleaded. “Look at this bricklaying. One good shove and it’ll come down.”

He took the steel rule from his back pocket and began to scrape at a central stone, causing the poorly mixed mortar to crumble to the floor. Five minutes later, he was able to shove the stone through the wall to create a window. Percy eagerly put his face up to the hole and shone his torch inside.

"What can you see?" asked David.

Percy remained silent.

"Come on Percy, what's in there?" repeated David impatiently.

Percy finally spoke, his voice no more than a whisper.

"I can see wonderful things!"

## CHAPTER 12

## Wonderful Things

The torch cavorted around the ink-black room like a World War Two searchlight looking for German bombers, pausing occasionally to examine the many gilded items, statuettes, piles of ancient furniture, jewellery, weapons, ceramic pots and ashabtis, all dwarfed by two huge sarcophagi. The room's walls were a rich, yellow ochre colour, quite unlike the rough sandstone of the tunnel, and covered in amazing, brightly-coloured hieroglyphics. David, who was getting a little annoyed with his stunned and silent employer hogging the view, shoved him to one side, snatched the torch and took a look for himself.

Now it was his turn to fall silent. The first glimpse of an undiscovered Egyptian tomb can do that to a person. Julian called them from the trapdoor, worried that they had both stopped talking, and fearing the worst. Awoken from his reverie by his curator's shouting, Percy assured him that all was well, and implored him to join them immediately. There followed a mighty mental battle between Julian the Fearful, hater of rats, dark tunnels and zombies, and Julian the Curator, lover of antiquities, fine art and all things Egyptian, and thankfully it was the latter who emerged victorious. Crossing himself like a good catholic, he took a deep breath, scampered down the ladder into the abyss and legged it as fast as he could in the direction of the torch light. After the obligatory five minutes of stunned silence, he finally spoke.

"Am I dreaming? Are we in the middle of some strange new reworking of Alice in Wonderland here, with Hitlerina playing the part of the white rabbit? Correct me if I'm wrong, but this is an ancient Egyptian burial chamber, situated in Tutton on Stour. This is surely not possible. We're near Kinver here, not Cairo, for God's sake."

"Beats me," agreed David breathlessly. He seemed to be in a state of deep shock, and could add nothing of substance to the debate.

Percy took another long look. "Folks, surely we have solved the mystery of Lord Henry Hickman's lost treasures. He may have disappeared abroad, but he left his treasures here, and they've been hidden for fifty years."

"You're right," agreed Julian. "He must have found this old tunnel and decorated it to make it look like a real burial chamber, so that he could display his artefacts in a realistic setting."

"I hate to disagree," chipped in David, "but that hardly seems likely does it? These nineteen-twenties archaeologists liked to display their stuff where visitors could see it, in proper glass cases in a trophy room. He could hardly invite his guests down a dank pit could he?"

"Maybe he just hid them down here when he did a runner, to avoid the creditors, hoping to return one day and reclaim the stuff," suggested Julian.

"Just like his recent relative tried to do, in fact!" added David.

"If that's so, why spend all that time decorating the walls with hieroglyphics?" asked Percy, perplexed. "One thing's for sure, the current Lord Hickman couldn't have known about the tunnel, or he'd have had a lot more than the Holbein drawing on his shopping list. This tunnel has not been entered since the nineteen-twenties. I'm sure of it."

“We need to knock this wall down,” said David. “I vote we borrow some sledgehammers from the builders, set up a few proper electric lights and get cracking.”

* * *

Julian’s excited dash from the building site to the library was interrupted by the sound of the telephone ringing in his office. He made a detour and breathlessly lifted the receiver. It was Constable Donald Bates, who’d rung to inform everyone that Herr Grunstrasse had been successfully detained at Twopenny Green Aerodrome, along with his swivel-eyed pilot, and they were currently trying to explain to Donald’s boss why they were in possession of a hundred and fifty thousand pounds in British currency, and, more worryingly, a Walther automatic pistol. Lord Hickman, meanwhile, was safely back in prison and presumably enjoying the first of many spiritual conversations with the Reverend Arthur Godisgood.

Shakespeare once wrote about sorrows not coming in single spies but in battalions, and it was pretty much the same kind of thing with Stanmore Castle phone calls. Had Shakespeare been born four hundred years later, he would no doubt have had something to say about buses too. The phone rang again, and this time it was Suzanne, requesting an interview with David. Julian caught David as he was about to disappear into the abyss with his borrowed hammer, so he reluctantly laid down his tool and trotted to the phone.

“It’s me!” said Suzanne cheerfully. Even the pickiest person could not have argued with that. She was perfectly correct in her assessment of the situation, and David told her so.

“How have you been without me then?” she continued.

"Okay!" replied David, somewhat preoccupied with the goings-on just down the corridor.

"Good of you not to ring me once while I've been away."

"That's always trickier when you don't leave me a phone number," argued David.

"Oh that's right, I knew it would end up being my fault," snorted Suzanne.

David loved the opposite sex, but had long given up trying to find any semblance of logic in their arguments. He let it pass without comment.

"The weather here is just beautiful. It's in the eighties, and we've got our own villa with a swimming pool. We're near a place called Els Poblets, which is a small town by the sea. Dad keeps calling it Hells Goblets."

"Great!" said David, vaguely. Julian was more than a little keen to begin, and was gesturing frantically at him to wind up the call.

"Have you been lonely without me then?"

"No," replied David, with his trademark tact. "Julian's living with me."

"Julian?"

"Yes. I work with him, and we make each other laugh, which is nice. He's wearing my clothes at the moment, because his house burnt down unexpectedly, and it's quite funny, because he's not the same shape as me at all."

"Are you having me on?"

"No. We cook dinner every night and everything. It's great!"

"Jesus David! You'll be telling me you're sleeping with him next."

"Well, funny you should say that....."

"Bloody hell! Why are they always called Julian? I was phoning to ask you if you'd mind my staying another week, but it sounds as if I should come straight back home on the next plane."

"No, no, don't do that. I can cope for another week if you'd like to stay," David assured her. "We'll be fine here. I must go because Julian needs me. We're about to knock an old wall down with sledgehammers."

"Oh right!" replied Suzanne, who was sounding a little dazed. "It's good to see that your Bachelor of Arts Honours degree wasn't wasted then."

The phone went dead. David was a very astute and sensitive young man, and something told him that his fiancée seemed off-hand; distant even. He vowed to probe her further when she next rang. He replaced the receiver and dashed back to the trap door with Julian, eager to begin.

The tunnel was hot and airless, with a damp, musty smell, and after half an hour of swinging the heavy sledgehammers, two of the three men were bathed in what is commonly referred to as the sweat of honest toil, whilst David, excused manual work due to his recent hernia operation, acted in a managerial and advisory capacity that was not universally welcomed.

They were all used to mental, rather than physical, exertion, and were it not for the fact that they did not want prying eyes anywhere near the tunnel, they would have been better served by offering the builders working on the tea rooms a few quid to do it for them. It was with feverish excitement that they finally cleared away the remaining stones, so that they could not only get into the chamber, but also have room to bring things out.

Percy, covered in brick dust and perspiration, was first to enter the room, followed by David, with Julian - who saw a direct correlation between the tomb and the recent spate of activity from The Undead - nervously bringing up the rear. The builders had lent them a long electrical cable attached to a light which was mounted on a tripod stand. The effect on the burial chamber was magical. By torchlight the room had teased and hinted at what it had to offer, but now the powerful floodlight revealed its true majesty.

Julian and David had both been fortunate enough to have visited the Tutankhamun exhibition when it visited London in nineteen-seventy-one, and remembered vividly the many solid gold treasures, inlaid with bright cobalt blue and terra cotta. They had marvelled at not only the exquisite craftsmanship, but also the condition of the artefacts, which looked as if they had been crafted a few weeks, rather than several thousand years, previously.

Seeing the treasures before them was even more thrilling, for whilst the individual pieces were obviously not as grand as those from Tutankhamun's tomb, the difference was that Percy's treasures were undiscovered, and strewn around as they had been left, back in the nineteen-twenties. The effect was broadly similar to walking into the type of antique shop that virtually every old town has, (usually owned by some wild-haired eccentric who hates to actually part with anything) which is full from floor to ceiling with all manner of dusty old relics, leaving very little floor space for the customers to navigate their way around the premises. The three men had to step carefully to avoid crushing the smaller items, such as the ancient children's toys, footstools and assorted ashabtis. There were small inlaid tables piled on top of larger inlaid tables, decorated boxes full of spears and bows, a one-man chariot, cooking pots, canopic jars, statuettes and tools galore, but their eyes were hypnotically drawn to two items that dwarfed the rest, and called out to be examined more closely.

Two huge sarcophagi lay side by side, covered in complex decorations and hieroglyphics. The slightly larger one appeared to have been made for a male, and the other for a female. Percy glanced at his two assistants, swallowed hard, and spoke with tremulous voice.

"We need to look inside, don't you think?"

"Bugger off!" replied Julian, the one who, if one will recall, laughed in the face of superstition. "Do you both realize what we have discovered here? These are almost certainly the burial caskets of Rametup and Sippahottut, if my brother's information is correct, which it will be, given what he does for a living. You know what he told us about the curse. Personally, I'd rather not crumble to dust just yet, if you don't mind."

"Total poppycock, Julian!" laughed Percy. "I'm surprised at an educated fellow like you, believing all that mumbo-jumbo."

David sprang to Julian's defence. "I know what you mean, Percy, but you weren't at the stables that night when the mummy in a black coat came up the stairs were you? Where's your logical explanation for that then? It scared the shit out of us!"

"Nothing more than anxiety," Percy assured them. "You'd wound yourselves up to hysteria level after Adrian's phone call and the pair of you were hallucinating, or having nightmares - one of the two. Now give me a hand with this lid, or you'll both be working somewhere else next week."

Percy began to try and manhandle the massive coffin lid by himself. Julian, who stood gormlessly watching whilst at least three conflicting emotions battled for pole position in his head, eventually bit the bullet and weighed in. David, medically exempt, shuffled from foot to foot and bit his nails to the quick. As the mighty sarcophagus front slid down, they were greeted by the mummified and bandaged head of Rametup, staring eerily back at them from within. Julian's face turned a ghostly grey, and he complained of feeling faint, meaning that David was forced to take over. After a few minutes sitting with his head between his legs and breathing deeply, Julian felt well enough to begin examining the objects around him, being particularly careful not to glance over at the mummy, just in case it set him off again.

Meanwhile, David and Percy slid back the lid of the second, smaller sarcophagus, and were greeted by similarly macabre contents.

"I think we'll slip the lids back on now," decided Percy. "It's enough to give you the heebie-jeebies. Let's take a look at the other stuff. I suppose we'll have to get it all up into the museum and catalogue it properly, eh Julian?"

Julian wasn't listening. He had been busying himself, clearing a space, and was staring into a small ante-room that he had discovered behind a pile of furniture.

"I've found something," he croaked, his throat so dry that he could barely speak. "It's another room. Get that light over here, quickly!"

The room was very small, measuring no more than ten feet square, with a very low ceiling. It had none of the intricate wall paintings that the other room had, and only a few canopic jars and spent candles scattered on the sandstone floor. What the room did have, however, was a large sarcophagus in the middle, with its lid removed and placed against the wall beside it. Draped over the lid was an old black coat, and lying in the sarcophagus was a sight so hideous that it caused Julian to dash from the small room and be violently sick in a three-thousand-year-old cooking pot.

The grotesque, distorted figure in the casket was only partly mummified. The head and upper body were wrapped loosely in bandage, as were the majority of the arms, and there had been some attempt made to begin the legs, but whatever had interrupted the vile task of preparing the body for the after-life had obviously been so traumatic that the embalmers had not returned to finish the job.

The bandaging around the head had come undone, leaving horrible empty eye sockets on view, and the areas of the hands and feet that were left unfinished had either become horribly shrivelled, or simply turned to bone. Several fingers, a thumb, and a toe or two were missing, presumed taken by a cat burglar. A small hole in the corner of the room leaked sunlight, and pointed the way to Hitlerina's entrance; a large plank of rough-hewn wood propped against the wall next to it providing the answer to how she'd ever managed to get out again with her odious prizes.

Julian was hyper-ventilating now, and needed to get upstairs in a hurry. Percy decided that they'd had quite enough excitement for the time being, and withdrew his troops to the surface for a cup of tea in the library. The tea seemed to do wonders for Julian, and quite soon the power of speech had returned, albeit shakily.

"God! That was horrible. I won't be able to sleep ever again. Did you see it, David? It was the mummy in the black coat that tried to get us over at the stables. This place is cursed, I'm sure of it now. After dark, that bastard down there rises from his box and haunts this castle. I'm out of here. I resign. Sorry folks; and I'm not working a week in hand either."

David said nothing, but just sat holding his elegant china tea cup and saucer, desperately trying to stop them rattling together.

Percy, the voice of reason, tried to reassure his staff. "Look, let's stay calm. You can't leave us, Julian. Remember what you said when you first arrived? This was the world's most boring museum. Well, it's not now! Just think what a fantastic place we'll have, once the exhibits are on display. We'll ditch the Museum of Local Life, and open the Stanmore Castle Museum of Egyptology. There's enough stuff down there to kit out the British Museum, *and* there's the small matter of an original Holbein drawing to take into consideration. That brother of yours will be bloody jealous of us before long. Take the week off and go on holiday. I'll pay. I'll buy you some clothes too, and you can rent a cottage in Kinver if you don't want to stay here overnight. I don't want a new curator. I've got used to you now. What do you say?"

Julian was touched. Percy just gawped at him imploringly with his head cocked to one side, like a lovesick spaniel.

"Okay!" he replied. "But I'm not staying after dark. Maybe we could call the vicar in and do an exorcism."

"Whatever you wish," agreed Percy. "But in the meantime, can you call your brother and let him know what we've found? No disrespect, but we need some specialist knowledge here."

* * *

Adrian Bytheway arrived with two of his staff on Monday afternoon, hot and sweating from a series of train journeys on a sweltering day. After catching up with his younger brother, greeting David like the favourite pen-pal he'd never met, and sipping tea with Percy in the library, they got down to the task in hand. The three white-coated, surgical mask-wearing British Museum staff disappeared below, armed with boxfuls of specialist equipment, only surfacing for refreshments, the occasional use of the telephone, and the odd lavatory visit. It was seven-thirty in the evening when two of the three Egyptologists finally hauled themselves back up, and summoned all concerned parties back to the library for their initial verdict.

"Well gentlemen," began Adrian grandly, milking the occasion for all it was worth. "We have some remarkable news. I took the liberty of borrowing your phone earlier, Percy; I hope you don't mind. I wanted to double-check something with Professor Aziz, who works at the Cairo Museum. He phoned me back an hour ago with some very interesting facts, and it confirmed what we had already discovered."

"Get on with it, Ade," demanded Julian impatiently. His elder brother gave him a withering look.

"Very well! Cairo has confirmed that they definitely have the mummies of Rametup and Sippahottut at their museum, but not their sarcophagi or treasures. These were spirited out of Egypt by none other than our friend, Lord Henry Hickman in the twenties. I didn't mention anything about who I was working for, incidentally, in case the buggers asked for their stuff back! Anyway, the two mummies in your main room below and the partially-mummified body in the small annexe have only been dead for around forty or fifty years, according to our mummy specialist, Doctor Bradley here, and he should know. It looks as if we have a mystery on our hands of Agatha Christie proportions, and I, for one, have never known anything like it. The good news, meanwhile, is that the artefacts are *definitely* more than fifty years old, and worth a fortune. You've probably gathered that our third member of staff, Professor Anton Porter, has not yet joined us. He's our hieroglyphics expert, so once he'd examined all the treasures, he volunteered to stay down there and decipher some of the wall writings. They're probably just gobbledegook, just to make the place look authentic, but you never know. He'll be joining us shortly for a cup of tea, and no doubt he'll fill us in then. Meanwhile gentlemen, you now have a sizeable and important collection, and we wouldn't mind a few of your bits and pieces at our place, to be honest! As to the mummies, I'm afraid we have to back off at this point. This is now a police matter."

Heads swivelled. David looked at Julian, who in turn looked at Percy, who was busy looking at David. Adrian chewed on a reflective Hobnob, while Doctor Bradley busied himself, removing particles from his fingernails.

David, as usual, was first to break the silence.

"Before anyone can ask the inevitable question, 'Well in that case, who are the three dead people in the bandages then?' let me give you my theory. I believe you have just been examining the bodies of Lord Henry Hickman, Lady Hickman, and Stokes, their loyal butler. After all, who else could it be? It all makes perfect sense. They were being hounded by creditors, and stood to lose the lot. Maybe they couldn't face the prospect of bankruptcy and disgrace, not to mention the actual loss of all their artefacts; the ones they'd spent a lifetime collecting, so they agreed to a suicide pact or something."

"What, the butler as well?" asked Adrian, unconvinced.

"Yes! Apparently, from what we have gleaned from old articles and so on, he followed them blindly wherever they roamed, and virtually dedicated his life to them. Lord Hickman was the roguish adventurer and collector, but don't forget that Lady Hickman was an eminent Egyptologist. Imagine them, like Hitler and Eva, trapped in the castle, with legal letters coming thick and fast. Instead of selling up and accepting their fate, they chose one last heroic gesture. The tunnel was probably there already, as we mentioned earlier, an escape route for priests and royalists. She decorated the place with authentic hieroglyphics and so on, he dragged all the stuff down there from the museum, aided and abetted by the loyal Stokes, and re-created Rametup and Sippahottut's tomb. Then they take a drink from a goblet full of Hemlock, or what-have-you, and die in each other's arms, but not before she has instructed old Stokes on how to embalm them. The faithful retainer does his duty, wraps them in bandage - I hope to God he didn't pull their brains down their noses with a sharp spike and put them in one of those canopic jars down there – and manhandles them into the two coffins. Then, his own life no longer having any meaning, he replaces the trapdoor, takes a candle and returns to his little annexe room, where he slips off his butler's coat and drinks the Hemlock, trying desperately and rather pathetically to wrap himself in bandage before he himself keels over. I can't see any other explanation for the half-hearted attempt at mummification and the coat draped over the lid, can you?"

"Bloody hell!" said Percy, spellbound, "You missed your vocation. You could have been Sherlock Holmes!"

"Thank you," replied David, sporting a superior smile. "Hand me my smoking jacket, my Stradivarius and a snort or two of opium will you, Julian? I intend to sum up, and as we all know, the part of the story where the detective does this sort of thing is always set in an oak-panelled library, so this is perfect. Gentlemen, I will be brief. The butler did it."

"Very amusing, I'm sure," added Julian. "But now we have to phone the police and get those dead bodies out of here. They give me the bloody creeps. Then, perhaps, this butler's soul will be laid to rest and he won't insist on scaring the living shit out of me anymore."

The conversation was interrupted by the arrival of a very animated and excited Professor Porter, who was covered in dust and sneezing violently into his handkerchief. Percy poured him a cup of tea, while he nervously opened his notepad and addressed the assembly.

"You are not going to believe this, folks!" he spluttered. "I have made the most incredible discovery. I've managed to decipher the writings on the walls, and you are not going to get your heads around what I have found out. The bodies downstairs are those of Lord and Lady Hickman and their loyal butler, Stokes...."

"Yeah, we know," interrupted Adrian. "Can I have another one of those Hobnobs, Percy?"

## CHAPTER 13

## An Inspector Calls

- One year later -

It was a glorious summer's day. Fluffy white clouds lounged about in a cobalt sky that was streaked with the merest hint of pink. Swifts performed their daring, Red Arrows-style air displays around the old farm buildings, watched by sedentary groups of wood pigeons who had seen it all before and were not impressed. The looming shadows of carp glided around in the reeds at the edge of the lake, keeping themselves to themselves, whilst the more energetic trout rippled the still waters in search of flies. God was in His Heaven, all was right with the world, and nowhere more so than at Stanmore Castle, near Tutton Common, South Staffordshire.

David was looking forward to seeing his old friends Percy and Adrian again, after a gap of six months. There had been many changes at the museum, and he was keen to catch up with gossip and talk about old times over a nice cup of tea in the library. What had begun as a few weeks of poorly-paid work while his hernia healed had turned into six months of solid employment and a remarkable period of his life that would never be forgotten.

The Museum of Local Life, with its mind-numbingly awful exhibits, had been confined to the pedal bin of history, and The Stanmore Castle Museum of Egyptology had risen triumphantly, Phoenix-like, from the ashes. There was, just for starters, a thriving tearoom and visitor's centre, which too had risen, quite literally, from the ashes of the stable block. There had been changes amongst the staff too. Jethro no longer tended to the flower beds or pushed wheelbarrows full of horse manure from point A to point B, and Glenda could no longer be seen struggling with huge silver tea trays laden with biscuits, thanks to Percy's kind hearted altruism. With the sale of one small but important artefact to The British Museum, he had financed the surgical work they both craved, with some woolly proviso that they should pay him back in small instalments, if they felt like it, once they had got their new lives in order.

There was a new company secretary working at the museum now, and unlike Glenda, she could type, spell, add up, answer the phone and liaise with the various schools and organizations that were falling over themselves to visit the place, now that the exhibits were worth seeing. She was also extremely easy on the eye; a factor that could not be overlooked in Percy's decision to employ her, though, surprisingly, she had not been his first choice. Originally, he had favoured Jane, the pneumatic-breasted barmaid from the Fox Inn, but had been out-voted by Julian, who put his foot down with a firm hand, pointing out that Jane, for all her attributes and personable nature, could only type seventeen words per day. This, he argued, was only marginally better than Glenda's personal best, though he had to admit that at least Jane spelled most of them correctly. A world class museum needed professional people, he insisted, and so it came to pass that Suzanne, David's fiancée, with her university education and Solihull accent, was duly appointed. This was indeed a shrewd move, as it meant David would retain an interest in the place, and could be called upon to provide cut-price artistic work when the occasion arose, in return for Percy helping to pay off David and Suzanne's mortgage.

David's first port of call was Julian's office, where he found the curator juggling two telephones. After he had dealt with the calls, he stood and welcomed David like a long lost brother.

"Where have you been?" he grinned. "It's too quiet around here without you!"

"Earning a living, Jools. I'd have loved to have stayed here forever, but Percy wouldn't bankroll it. I've got an illustrator's agent now, and I'm doing some great work. My stuff is appearing on album sleeves, postage stamps, paperback covers, jam labels, you name it."

"I know. I hear it all from Suzanne, your mole within our organization. She's over at the gift shop, keeping an eye on some little horrors from a local school, by the way."

"Is she, Bytheway?"

"Yes, very amusing - never heard that one before. Well, you'll be pleased to know your murals have been a great success, though it pains me to compliment you so. Your recreation of Rametup's tomb is just stunning. It's the room that all the visitors like best. We've added the Lord and Lady Hickman waxworks since you last came, and darkened the room, with the figures holding lanterns, as if they've only just discovered the treasures. It looks fantastic, and adds a real sense of drama to the tableau, just like it was down in the tunnel when we found the stuff. We're also getting thousands of people visiting the Holbein room to see the Lady Jane Grey picture. The boss pulled off a masterstroke there you know. It was a big blow, us having to return the real drawing to its rightful owner, especially right after the police had made Percy give up the mummies for burial. I think he was dead set on displaying them, but health and safety were having none of it. Neither was I, incidentally. Good riddance I say, and we've had no more zombie sightings since! Anyway, his brainwave saved the day, I must admit. The owner of the drawing didn't particularly want anyone knowing what he'd got stashed away in the safe at his house, and he was so grateful that Percy had offered to return it without a fuss that he allowed the museum to *pretend* that the one on its wall was the original - a deal that suited both parties! Incidentally, the bloke phoned me the other day with a technical question about his original drawing, but I'm afraid I couldn't answer it. I promised I'd get onto Ade at the British Museum and get back to him."

"What did he want?" asked David, a little skittishly.

"Oh, it was just something about how Holbein catalogued his drawings."

"Meaning?"

"Well, he's noticed a small number in pencil on the back of the drawing, and he wondered what it meant, that's all."

"What number?" David's throat felt very dry. He took a sip of Julian's Evian water. "I might know the answer."

"Oh right! I think he said there was a number thirty-five and then a letter 'P'."

The next gulp of Evian water bypassed his oesophagus and cascaded into his lungs, causing a dramatic choking fit. Julian stood and thumped his back heavily, an action which was both extremely painful and completely ineffectual. When reason was eventually restored to its throne, David continued.

"A thirty-five, followed by the letter 'P' you say. That was, erm … Holbein's way of numbering his drawings. It stands for Pencil Drawing number thirty-five. He numbered them all like that."

Julian eyed him suspiciously, and then turned his attention back to his diary, where he had been organizing his various school events. After a few seconds of silence, interrupted only by the sound of a penny dropping, he slowly lifted his head and gazed at David with a look of utter disbelief.

"You never did."

"What?"

"You *did*, didn't you? I think I need to go and study Percy's Holbein again."

"I don't know what you're on about!"

There was a tap on the door, which had the same therapeutic effect on David that the 'End of Round One' bell has on a boxer who is getting seven shades of excrement punched out of him. Jessica, the new cleaner and tea lady, appeared with refreshments for them both.

"Thanks Jess," said David. "I'm glad you remembered the Hobnobs."

"Julian remoinded me that you loiked 'em, Mister Dave," she said, and withdrew shyly from the room.

Sensing that Julian might wish to carry on probing where he'd left off, David hastily made his excuses and proceeded, teacup in hand, to the main exhibition room, where Percy was holding court, showing around a small group of American tourists. Not wishing to interrupt his old employer in mid flow, he sat gazing out of the window at the castle grounds. It was gratifying to see the old place in good hands now, and obviously thriving.

The lawns, which were at one time neglected and threadbare, were now manicured and striped once more. Peacocks strutted around, wailing like banshees, and the newly-appointed, heavily-tattooed gardener strode purposefully from point A to point B with a wheelbarrow full of horse shit. Gaggles of visitors sat at the picnic tables in the courtyard licking their ice creams contentedly, and the gift shop seemed to be doing a roaring trade in outsized pencils, Tutankhamun pencil tins, colouring books, Fez hats and hundreds of other Egyptian-themed pieces, all hand-crafted, gilded in twenty-four carat gold paint and guaranteed to beautify and enhance the home.

The Cairo Café was also teeming with punters, eager to try the 'Shrivelled Mummy Fingers and Mash', a cocktail sausage-based concoction dreamt up by Julian which was a winner with the school parties, especially when served with a strawberry flavoured 'Ashabti Milk-Sheik', or perhaps a 'Sippahot-Cup' hot chocolate drink.

David watched with great interest as an American child, unimpressed with the English fayre, tried to offload a Mummy Finger to the small black and white cat beneath his picnic table, only to see the fussy animal refuse the offer and try her luck elsewhere. Hitlerina had tasted the real thing, after all, and would accept no substitutes. The child's obese father, returning from the café laden with several King Tut-Burgers, French fries and buckets of Diet Coke, turned and smiled benignly at the little moustachioed cat as it sidled past, and immediately tripped over a twelve stone, sleeping Labrador, sending the tray and its contents flying in all directions across the cobbled court yard.

Inside the exhibition room, Percy was still in full flow, and summoned David to join in and take a bow.

"This," said Percy proudly, "is the very man I was telling you about. The artist who designed all of our tableaux."

"Pleased to meet you, sir!" said the large American lady. "You did a great job here. We were visiting Anne Hiawatha's Cottage in Stafford upon Avon, and our tour guide recommended that we take a detour to see your lovely castle and museum. I can tell you that it was worth the trip. We had lunch at The Whittington Inn, where Dick Whittington and his wife, Lady Jane Grey lived, so that was very special."

"I love The Whittington," said David. "They say that some of the food there is hundreds of years old."

"It was fabulous, honey," gushed the lady, "but this place is even better. It's hard to believe that these mummies are *thousands* of years old. The bandages are a little brown and stained, but other than that, the bodies could have been wrapped up six months ago!"

"It's tea that causes the brown stains," grinned David. Percy gave him one of his looks.

"You Brits are all comedians!" laughed the lady. "I don't think mummies drank tea."

"They did before you lot threw it all in the river," explained David. This appeared to fly about a yard over the American lady's head. Sensing that she was going down a cul-de-sac with this strange young man, she turned to Percy in the hope that he might be a tad more lucid.

"So, are these the actual bodies of Rametup and his wife, Sippahottut?"

"Unfortunately not," explained Percy. "They are in the museum in Cairo, but these are mummies from the same period, and were probably members of the royal family."

The lady was spellbound. "Goodness! Do you know who they were?"

"Yes," said Percy, glancing at David with a twinkle in his eye. "That one there is, erm, Eltun-efertiti, and that one is Tarbukahmun. The one in the plainer sarcophagus is, erm, Samijunises. The hieroglyphics revealed that he was Tutankhamun's official song and dance man, apparently."

The American lady's fat and freckled ten-year-old son piped up. "I never heard of 'em."

"That's fair enough son," frowned Percy, "but they were all very well-known in their day."

"And is that Lord Hickman and his wife, holding the lanterns?" asked the lady. "They seem familiar."

"A lot of folks mention that," said Percy.

The American lady's even fatter friend chipped in.

"He looks like Lord Lucan. The man who was supposed to have killed his nanny and disappeared."

Percy had to agree that there was a certain likeness. He explained that most of the British aristocracy were all descended from the same source, so these likenesses were quite common.

"Accepted," nodded the second American lady, "But she's familiar too. It's on the tip of my tongue. Am I thinking of an entertainer? A singer maybe?"

"Ah, you mean Shirley Bassey!" replied Percy. "It's been commented on before actually. Lady Hickman was Welsh you see. Apparently, she was Shirley Bassey's grandmother's step-sister, on the paternal side, so the resemblance is no coincidence. Well spotted!"

The American ladies' already ample bosoms swelled with pride. "Just call me Miss Marple!" said the fatter one. "Nothing gets past me!"

"There's very little room," whispered David, to no one in particular.

The new gardener burst into the room, looking flustered. He apologized for interrupting Percy's conversation, but explained that there was a man at the front door that looked like Captain Mainwaring from Dad's Army, who said he was the Museum's Inspector for the West Midlands, and was asking to speak to the owner. Percy made his excuses to the American party and dashed out of the main exhibition room towards the front door.

A short, officious-looking character in a three-piece suit stood impatiently on the steps, obviously a little miffed that the gardener had not invited him in.

"Good afternoon!" said Percy. "How can I be of service?"

"My name is Hubert Billingham," said the little man, with a rather snooty tone. "I am the government's Museum's Inspector for the Midlands area."

"I know!" smiled Percy. "Glenn the gardener just told me. I'm sorry if he didn't invite you in. He's excellent with horse manure

- none better in fact, but a little lacking in the social graces. I expect you have to inspect the old place with a view to awarding us stars and whatnot. Am I correct?"

"Exactly so. Yes."

"Excellent. Excellent! Well walk this way, Mr Billingham. I think we'll start with the store cupboard."

*The End.*

**Books in the David Day Series.**

**A NASTY BUMP ON THE HEAD**

Eleven-year-old David Day finds the curmudgeonly toy shop owner, Miss Kettle, murdered in her shop. He duly informs Scotland Yard, only to bump into her in Tenbury-Wells the following week.

**MONET TROUBLE**

First year art student David Day is persuaded to forge a Monet painting by the mysterious Lord Hickman, but unknown to either of them, several other artists have the same idea.

**VINCENT GOUGH'S VAN**

An art college murder mystery of Shakespearian proportions, littered with psychic sewing teachers, entrail-painting students and lesbian assassins.

**THE CURSE OF TUTTON COMMON**

David sets about trying to improve Britain's worst museum, and ably assisted by a cat named Hitlerina, he discovers an ancient Egyptian tomb in South Staffordshire.

**Written and soon to be published;**

**PAINTING BY NUMBERS**

Thirty-year-old David is having a mid-life crisis, made worse by the fact that his art studio has exploded, and the ninety-year-old 'paint by numbers' enthusiast he has befriended is not what he seems.

**STEALING THE ASHES**

Forty–year-old David Day overhears two Australian cricketers plotting to steal the Ashes, and, ably hampered by his best friend Laz, he tries his best to thwart their plans.

**THE HUNT FOR GRANDDAD'S HEAD**

The prequel to Nasty Bump! Daleks have invaded Brierley Bank, but David harnesses their power to see off the neighbourhood bully.

**...and a new novel featuring a new hero!**

**THE CURIOUS TALE OF THE MISSING HOOF**

Writer Adam Eve hires a pantomime horse costume, but forfeits his deposit when he loses one of the hooves. His obsessive efforts to locate it create mayhem!

For more information, email gt@geofftristram.co.uk

Those of you who have read a David Day book will know how addictive they can become. At first, you think you can take them or leave them – you are an adult with a modicum of willpower, after all, and no mere book is going to rule your life. Quite soon though, you realize that you've started reading a quick chapter while you're in the bath or the lavatory. From there it is but a short step to the torch under the bed sheets at midnight and the paperback hidden inside your desk at the office. You'll find yourself reading the final chapter extra slowly to make it last longer, savouring every word and even reading good bits twice. Then, when you can stall no further and the book is finished, you will go through an awful mourning process, whereupon an intense craving will kick in. You'll need more and you'll need it NOW. Bad-tempered due to the crippling withdrawal symptoms, you'll probably complain that the author isn't nearly prolific enough for your voracious appetite, and begin to call him rude names. Extreme cases have even been known to try and climb the walls in anguish. Friends will turn against you because you will insist on regurgitating the plots *ad nauseam* while they're trying to watch television. It will get so bad that you might seriously consider a spell in a rehab clinic, or maybe a course of hypnotism.

Well, help is at hand. Why not join the David Day Fan Club? It's a bit like Alcoholics Anonymous. You sit around in a circle and confess, "My name is Deirdre Sponge and I'm a David Day fanatic." (Obviously, you don't say this if your name *isn't* Deirdre Sponge. That was just an example.) Then the others get up and hug you, with a bit of luck.

If you email me at gt@geofftristram.co.uk I'll keep your name on file and let you know when a new book is due to be released into the wild. Unlike other authors who are now too important – people such as J.K. Rowling and William Shakespeare for example, I promise to be approachable, grateful, humble, and always write back. That's with the proviso that you tell me my books are great, of course. I don't want any sour-faced old scrooges writing in to tell me I'm rubbish and that I deserve to be horse-whipped on the steps of my club. Maybe I could cope if you've spotted a glaring error, or a bit you didn't think made perfect sense, but obviously, I'd prefer it if you to told me how a paragraph had made you wet yourself on the train, or prevented you from leaping off a high building to certain death. You can suggest things that David can get up to in future stories, if you wish. I might even write *you* into a book. After all, most of my characters are based on real people, believe it or not! Oops! Shouldn't have admitted that – now no one will believe that legal disclaimer in the small print at the beginning.

Anyway, I'll leave it with you. The offer's there. You can lead a horse to water but you can't make it drink, as my Granny Bertha often tried to say. I hope you've enjoyed 'The Curse of Tutton Common'. It's 'Painting by Numbers' next, and if *that* doesn't make you laugh, I'll refund your money.

That was a joke by the way. You have to be so careful in this litigious age. I need the money for a new conservatory - I can't afford to give it back. The bookshops keep forty percent anyway. And another thing - will you stop lending my books to everyone when you've finished them? Let them buy their own. I'm never going to be another J.K. Rowling at this rate.

*Geoff Tristram.*